# night shift

nightSHADE

# carey decevito

*For all who soldier on despite what life throws at them...*
*May you find your happiness.*

# *acknowledgments*

First and foremost, where would I be without the unconditional support of my family. This one was a tough one to get through with all the hurdles we had to jump over. Thank you for understanding the times I've had to hole myself in some quiet corner to get things done, for cheering me on, and being as excited as I was that I finally typed those two little words.

Eric David Battershell—your impeccable talent and undying friendship went a long way in capturing Shane for this amazing cover.

Burton Hughes—my Shane, my friend, my brother from another mother. Your friendship and support means the world to me.

Karen Hrdlicka—girl, we've had our fair share of getting this one just right and on time. Thank you for the laughs and your amazing insight to make Shane's story a reality.

Joanne Thompson—you're a friend first and foremost, but your support and recommendations have deemed you indispensable in my little book world. You are my proofreader extraordinaire.

My dearest Betas—without you, I wouldn't be able to put this or any of my books out. Your insight, opinions and dedication are immeasurable and I will forever appreciate having you all in my corner.

Bloggers, readers & fellow authors—the book community is one that can sometimes be easy to get lost into. Thank you for your support, your continued readership, and most of all, providing me with the kick in the ass I've most definitely needed. I try my best to support and share everything out there, and it definitely doesn't go unnoticed that you pay it forward.

*prologue*

"WHAT ARE YOU DOING HERE?" The tension around me palpable, she hurried aside to let me enter before closing the door behind us.

My blood boiled.

My skin crawled that she'd let *him* do that to her.

I had to get rid of it.

The taint.

Purify her.

"What have you done? You're mine, Evie. I told you, when I came back, you'd be mine and now look at yourself." Disgust was as clear in my voice as it was in my expression.

"Wh—whatever it is…we can talk this out," she stuttered, her feet inching her backward as I followed her movements.

Reaching to the small of my back, my fingers wrapped around the grip as I pulled it from its sheath. The eight-inch blade caught the glint of the afternoon sun, mesmerizing me, causing me to admire the play of light against it before I focused on the woman before me.

Her eyes shone with terror. "You don't…" She shook her head left to right, swallowing hard, stumbling against the side table next to the sofa. "You don't have to do this." She righted herself. "We can still be together. Now that...now that you're back—"

I shot her an incredulous look. Did she think me a fool? "You've gone and done the unthinkable. You had his child!" I hollered, my knuckles gripping the knife tightly. "This is the only way...the only way to get rid of the stain."

Her steps froze momentarily. "*Stain*?"

"It's what I should have done a while ago," I spat, cornering her as her steps were halted by the wall at her back. "What you took from me...what should have been mine," I raged, "is what I'll take from you."

One moment my eyes darted toward the hallway where I knew the devil lay in slumber, and the next, Eva Peters was making a mad rush toward the door that separated me from saving us all.

"No!" she panted. "You're crazy!"

If she only knew. "Move, Evie," I growled, "it's the only way."

"She's not here. Please!" Tears streamed down her face, her body shaking with fear.

Using the tip of the blade, I ran it over her soaked cheek, the metal sharp enough to catch on her ivory skin, causing a streak of blood to suddenly materialize.

I felt lighter instantly.

Powerful.

In control. A feeling I hadn't had in quite some time.

Manning my knife, I proceeded to run the tip of it down to her bottom lip, nicking it just enough for another bubble of her essence to form.

"Mmm..." I groaned, leaning forward to press my front against hers, taking the time to lick her damaged lip, then whispered my new realization while rubbing my impossibly hard cock against her stomach. "I was wrong. This..." I ran my finger through the blood on her cheek, watching its movement, "is what I need, Evie."

. . .

The sadness was overwhelming as I stared at the beauty laying limp and lifeless beneath me.

The rage I'd felt had all but dissipated with each slice of my blade through her flesh. Like a hot knife through butter, each time blood began to pour out, a weight lifted within me.

What once held pleading in her eyes, was now long gone.

She was nothing but a piece of art, trussed up by her silk scarves, a vessel conveying my message.

I'd be back...

*one*

Shane

## *EIGHT YEARS LATER*

THE MOMENT I walked over the threshold, I knew a clusterfuck of epic proportion awaited me.

Blood was everywhere. Spatter by the front door, smears over the walls, and droplets leading to where I knew the victim would ultimately be laying in a pool of her life's essence.

Forensics was going to have a field day with this one.

*Just like with the other fifteen.*

Donning the protective gear the lead officer had ordered me to change into before entering the scene, I made my way toward the back of the house.

Carefully avoiding one evidence marker after another, I entered the master bedroom. The grizzly sight of Victoria Spark's mutilated body, lying face up on the bed, greeted me. The standard ligatures on her wrists and ankles proved she'd been restrained and alive through most of her torture; the killer leaving her to die in excruciating pain from her wounds, and ultimately, blood loss.

The scent of copper in the air thickened as I made my final approach, slipping my hands into a pair of latex gloves. I was looking for something I knew was meant for me.

Setting my evidence kit down beside the bed, I bent toward the body in search of my next clue.

The sickening crack of the victim's jaw set my stomach to roiling as I pulled her mouth open, locating the three pieces I had come to expect after so many years of chasing this perp. Letting go of the victim, I grasped my digital camera and photographed my findings. Setting the camera down, I whipped out the small evidence bag from my kit and opened it, manning my tweezers.

Fishing the objects out one by one, I dropped them into the bag, then photographed them again. Fragments of a photograph were what this sicko left. Camera in hand, I shot a few frames of the room, as well as the rest of the premises. The team would have their own photos, but I liked being thorough with my investigations, thus preferred gathering my own shots, comparing them with the others.

Closing up my kit, I stood to take my leave.

*Fucking sadistic bastard and his games.*

It pissed me off that he was always one step ahead of me.

Thinking on those tiny pieces—the unknown subject, or unsub's calling card—I was confused more than ever as to why he was leaving them at every scene. The letter I'd received at the precinct, a week after the first murder, had alluded that they were all part of some demented countdown...a puzzle of sorts. One thing was clear however, the perp was after me, and after sixteen murders, I still wasn't any closer to finding this guy.

In my career as a detective, I'd come across a lot of questionable characters. I'd done my fair share of arresting the dregs of society and making enemies along the way. You couldn't be a cop without that happening.

"I take it that Rosie is in for another disappointing birthday dinner?" Will asked, coming to a stop at my side as I exited the victim's home.

Two days a year, I dealt with this bullshit; one being my daughter's birthday, the other was a day I'd rather forget entirely.

For the last eight years, it had been the same fucking story. That in itself was enough to confirm that the unsub was gunning for me. That, and the fact he'd started this spree of his, claiming none other than my wife as his first victim.

My main problem was my list of suspects lacked in possibilities. This perp was meticulously careful. He treated his kills as if they were some kind of gruesome artwork: from the placement of limbs to the blood spatter surrounding them—even those fucking, godawful puzzle pieces.

"I hate going back on my promise," I growled. "She's going to be pissed."

"I know it's your case, Shane, but I'm your partner," Will said. "Take a few hours, go to her, then come back if you have to."

I nodded. "I have what I need right now. You sure you can handle everything without me?"

He patted me on the back as I straightened from the body and backed away. "I'll call if something comes up. And I'll handle the FBI."

Thanking him, I handed him my evidence bag, then made to leave the scene, my camera and evidence kit in tow.


Caught up in old memories, I drove home on autopilot, scenes from eight years ago playing in my head.

The same black hair. The same look of terror, frozen in her open eyes.

Eva had been bound too.

And cut up.

Blood. God! There'd been so much blood everywhere.

I'd been the one to find her. I hated to think what would have been had my Rosie been there that day.

"Daddy!" was squealed, knocking me out of my grizzly thoughts.

Opening the car door and letting myself out, I caught her as she launched herself into my arms.

My princess.

The light of my life.

Buffing my cheek against my now nine-year-old's hair, then kissing it, I looked toward the house to find my mother standing there, a smile of pride, but the worry and apprehension she'd come to feel over the years—on this day—was evident in her eyes.

"Happy birthday," I rasped. "Did you have a good day at school? But most importantly, are you ready for dinner?"

Rosie reared her head and looked at me in shock. "We're still going?"

Smiling, despite feeling my heart breaking at my parental failings, I nodded. "We sure are."

Passing my mother as I carried my daughter over the threshold, I gave her inquisitive look a slight nod to confirm her suspicions, only to hear her curse under her breath.

It wasn't like I could hide it from the woman. She was a junky for news, and there was no way that this latest murder was going to stay out of it. It's as if they had set reminders on their calendars on the exact dates with the way that shit hit the TV and radio stations, and don't get me started on the print and digital media.

Following the women out to the car, I paused to watch Emberlyn, our neighbor, staring down at a package in her hand. She looked pale. Paler than her usual ivory complexion.

Before I could stop her, my daughter made a beeline for the other side of the street. "Ember! Ember! It's my birthday and

Daddy's taking us out!" I could feel her excitement radiating off her in waves.

Considering I was standing in the driveway, and my daughter had basically yelled her news to the entire neighborhood, I didn't get to hear what Emberlyn had to say. I simply watched as the woman nodded to me in greeting, bent down to my daughter with a smile covering that troubled look I'd seen moments before, and kissed her cheek.

Looking at my watch, I hated myself for feeling rushed. "Lana Rose, we need to go, baby girl."

Her nose scrunched up as she turned to look at me. "I'm not a baby!" Turning with a smile for the woman standing next to her, the one whose eyes were now trained on me, she nearly lost her balance when my daughter tackled her with a hug. "I'll see you later, Ember," she yelled, pausing to look to both sides of the street before running back to me. My eyes followed my girl's progress as she jumped in the back seat of my Escalade before I looked back toward my neighbor.

"Enjoy dinner," she called in place of goodbye.

Jutting my chin out in acknowledgment, I turned toward my family and got in the driver's seat.

"Do you think they'll have cake?" Rosie asked, making my mother laugh.

Their giggles had me grinning from ear to ear. My day could use a few more lighthearted moments.

I turned, giving her a wink. "I'm sure they can swing it, Princess."

"Ember said she'll show me how to make lip gloss, Daddy!"

As the evening went on, trying to stay focused on a nine-year-old's girlie interests got harder.

Mom nudged me to get me out of my head.

"What did you say, Princess?"

My mind was on the woman who'd lost her life, due to a

vendetta against me. It was also on the night when I lost my wife. When my daughter lost her mother.

"I get to make lip gloss with Ember," Rosie announced.

Hugging her into my side, I kissed the top of her head. "That's great, honey, but make sure that if I'm not around, that Grams knows where you're headed, alright?" I made a mental note to look Emberlyn up as soon as I had more time. The woman seemed harmless enough to me, but unlike with my other neighbors, who Mom knew, since we moved in with her after we'd lost Eva, Emberlyn was the proverbial new kid in town, only having lived there for a couple of years.

"I promise," she declared, crossing her finger over her heart. "You'd like her, Daddy."

I snorted while Mom was trying to stifle a snicker. "What makes you say I don't?" I couldn't say I liked or disliked her; I didn't know her all that well.

My little girl shrugged her shoulders. "You never talk to her. She's funny, and silly, and she makes cotton candy things. Well, not out of cotton candy, but her lip gloss sure tastes good! The other day, she dropped off some lotion for Grams' birthday and gave me a tube of her stuff, too. Grams thinks she's sweet."

"She did, huh?" I asked, looking from my daughter to my mother, who was sporting an amused smirk. She confirmed this with a slight nod.

"She's a little shy, but she's a complete sweetheart," Mom said. "Honestly, I don't see much of her. She's always so busy in that little cottage behind her place, and when she's not, she's always leaving her front door all gussied up, with a new shipment of her products to deliver."

With both the women in my life displaying such open interest in the woman, curiosity got the best of me. Leaning onto my elbow, my chin in my hand, I asked, "What does she do? I've heard lotion and lip gloss."

"She makes different kinds of all-natural products," Mom said. "Lotions, shampoos, makeup, soaps, salves, essential oils.

The woman is a genius if you ask me. She's a little crafty, too and has been working on this new line of candles. She told me she really enjoys pottery, just last week, too."

Through all of this, Rosie nodded in agreement. "You should see it, Dad. It's pretty cool. It's like cooking or baking, but with stuff you get to wear." The look of wonderment in her eyes had me laughing. It looked like Ms. Emberlyn Roth, had both females' approval, and I'd be lying if I said that part of me hadn't noticed the way she was with both of them, or how her looks affected me.

Changing the subject, I smiled and turned to my daughter. "Are you ready for some cake?"

*two*

Emberlyn

I WAS TINKERING in the garden when I heard the car roll up the drive, but I paid it no attention.

I'd been neighbors with the Peters going on two years now. Ever since my grandmother left me her house in her will. It had been the best and smartest decision for me. I'd needed a change of pace, a different locale, and living where I've felt safest all my life had an appealing draw that I simply couldn't ignore.

"Ember!" I heard Lana Rose call out. "I have cake!"

Leaving my bowl of cut blooms on the ground, I wiped my hands onto my already soiled jeans and stood, looking her way. The kinks in my back stretched and popped from their stiffness of being crouched on the ground for so long.

"Lucky girl," I called out.

"Did you want some?"

Fuck, the child had found my weakness, but I wasn't going to let her in on it. "No," I smiled, "but thank you, sweets."

"Okay, bye!" Running inside, I realized Shane was still staring at me, a quirking of his lips the only indicator that he was humored by our exchange. The rest of him was rock solid, dominating...and assessing.

With a quick wave of my hand as both hello and goodbye, I bent to pick up my tools and the bowl I used to collect the blooms I needed for the new batch of essential oils I was fixing to get started on. When I looked back from my front door, the man was gone.

I'd just finished setting the oils to the side for cooling when my doorbell rang.

No one came calling these days, except for the mailman and assorted courier services.

*And my ex, apparently.*

Since my front door was one of those solid wood numbers with an arched top without windows, I used the small window at its side to see who my visitor was.

Shane Peters.

Well, Shane's back to be more precise.

*Shit.*

Instantly, my mind started whirling. Had I done something wrong? I had been spending more time with his daughter lately, maybe he just thought it was weird and wanted to warn me off. I mean, it is weird, right? Or maybe he wanted to buy some lotion. Studying the man for a little longer, I wasn't quick enough to quell the bubbling laughter that trickled out of me. He didn't look like the type of man to use lotion. Then again, what would I know?

Finally, getting a hold of my bout of hilarity, I reached for the doorknob and opened the door.

The man turned and whatever remained of my humor fled as I took the whole of him in.

I'd never seen him up close like this.

His dark blond hair was a little messy, probably from running his hands through it. He wore his badge, which told me he was most likely heading back to work. He worked a lot from what Nora, Shane's mother, and Lana Rose had told me. Then again, so did I.

Aside from the black dress shirt and the faded denim he sported, his feet were encased in black boots. How he got that shirt to fit over his beefy shoulders and arms was beyond me, but the entire look had my mouth watering; and so did the slice of cake he was holding.

"Hey." His voice was smooth. "What's so funny?"

"N—nothing," I stuttered, feeling like an idiot.

"Did I catch you at a bad time?" he asked, his eyes studying me.

All I could do was shake my head, no.

"Here." Handing me the paper plate with the slice of cake, I took it and stared at the tasty-looking morsel. "Your mouth said no, but your eyes told the truth. You weren't imposing, by the way."

"I...Thank you, that's really kind of you." I turned to set the plate on the table next to the door, still standing on the threshold.

He shrugged his shoulders. "No problem."

My, "Would you like to come in?" came at the same time as his, "I should go." We both ended up smiling at one another, and I could feel heat rising in my face.

"Be safe," I bade him. "At work, I mean. You are heading to work, right?" I really should learn how to talk to hot men. Then again, being thirty-three, I doubted you could teach me that trick. If I ever entertained the thought of settling down again, whoever the person was would have to take me as I was.

His smile was tight, his eyes darkening. "Yeah." Turning, he walked down my front steps and turned when he reached the walkway. "Have a good night, Emberlyn." Not waiting on my reply, he waved, crossed the street at a slow jog, then jumped in his car and left.

"Thanks for the cake," I whispered, as I watched his tail-lights fade into the distance.

Closing the door and locking it, I grabbed the small plate, and headed for the kitchen. I jumped up to sit on my island countertop, reached over to grab a fork out of the drawer, then set to remove the plastic wrap before digging in. The decadence of the chocolate cake had me moaning and forgetting about my troubles, sitting on the same surface I was on, only a mere few feet away. Instead, I daydreamed about a certain blond detective stud who lived across the street, wondering what my current indulgence would taste like if it were smeared onto various parts of his body.

# *three*



WILL WAS WAITING for me at the precinct when I arrived.

"So? Catch me up." I came to a stop in front of his desk.

The man grabbed the case file and pushed it toward me. "Haven't got the report from the medical examiner's office yet, but let's face it, Shane...this is the same guy."

I perused the photos in there, trying to see if I could find something different from all the other cases. My eyes burned from exhaustion. My head hurt from trying so hard to make all of the pieces come together.

"That's all we've got?" I asked.

"'Bout it."

"Did you canvass the neighborhood to see if anyone saw anything?" I asked.

"Nothing." Will looked about just as frustrated as I felt. "Fucker's always hitting suburbia, where everyone works outside of the home. Vic's boyfriend said he left yesterday morning to fly out to Vegas for a conference. He last spoke to her this morning when she was heading into work." I nodded, looking at his case notes. Everything there matched what he was telling me.

"There's no reason for her to have gone home then?"

"Nothing but a text from an unknown number," he said. "Her boss said that she'd left in a hurry. A few coworkers noticed the same thing."

"Was the phone traced?"

Our eyes met. Dead end. "Phone was a burner. He ditched it in an alleyway behind the Walmart on Western Boulevard."

"And the text?"

"Same story about the partner wanting to meet," Will gritted out. "Part of me thinks these women know this man, or at least he seems trustworthy enough to them. I mean, they live in populated areas, they're always found in their beds in the same manner. A settled woman wouldn't bring in just any John off the street into their homes, right?"

"Mmm. Right."

*And they all look like my dead wife,* I added internally to the list of victim commonalities we'd established.

I sighed. "We keep waiting for this guy to slip up, but I'm thinking this isn't going to happen until he comes for me, Will."

The man groaned. "I know it feels that way, but there has to be something we're missing."

I shoved everything back into the file and closed it. "Do you mind if I take this home with me? I need some sleep, but I want a closer look at things, see if I can figure out his angle."

"Sure, man," he said. "I'm heading that way now, too. The FBI are going over everything we've put together so far. So, how'd dinner go with Little Miss Rosie?"

I grinned. "Fuck, does that kid light up my life," I told him, making him grin. "It was great. Had dinner with my two favorite ladies." *And had somewhat of a conversation with my gorgeous neighbor, for the first time since she's moved to the neighborhood,* I added to myself.

Getting up from his desk chair, I followed his move to leave.

"I'm glad for you." Will's pat landed on my shoulder with a quick squeeze.

"Thanks for pulling relief, brother. Breaking another promise would have killed me," I grumbled, and ran my hand through my messy hair before scrubbing my face. "I feel like a failure with this whole parenting shit. Rosie doesn't even ask me for a birthday party anymore. She told me that she knows that my work is important, and that if I got called in, then there wouldn't be a party anymore and everyone would have to go home early." Mom would have been there to look after things if I got called away, but the truth of the matter hurt. She didn't care that her friends would have been there to celebrate with her. She wanted me. End of story.

After I got home, the first thing I did, once I'd checked that all the windows and doors were locked, was look in on Rosie. She was tucked in safely and sound asleep. Crouching down, my fingers reached to push the hair covering the side of her face, brushing it aside as I leaned down, kissing my princess. She looked so much like her mother it was almost painful to look at her.

"Goodnight, baby," I whispered before standing upright.

Leaving her room, I made my way to the liquor cabinet in the kitchen, grabbed a tumbler, and poured myself four fingers of whiskey, stashing the bottle before taking my glass in hand.

"I saw what you did earlier." My mother crept into the kitchen, grabbing herself a bottle of water from the fridge. She turned to face me, a smirk on her face. "That was nice of you."

"She wanted cake, but she was too shy to admit it, so I brought her cake, Mom. That's it."

"Mm-hmm."

"Mom," I warned, my gaze assessing her with a prickle of suspicion niggling the back of my neck. "What's going on?"

"You should really think about putting yourself out there."

I rolled my eyes. "Not this again."

"She's a really nice girl, Shane."

Taking a hefty gulp of the amber liquid, I let the burn come as I swallowed it. "I know she's nice, Mom."

"But?" she prompted.

"Look...I'm just not ready yet."

"Are you sure about that?" Her eyes narrowed on me. "You looked damn ready to me, with that bounce in your step as you left to go meet up with Will earlier."

It was time for me to walk away and close out this conversation. "Mom, I don't want to talk about this. I date, and that's enough for me right now, but what I'm also telling you is that I will find my own dates, on my own time, and at my own convenience. Drop the matchmaking act."

Her eyes softened and tears filled them. "I miss her too, sweet boy," she whispered, hugging herself. "She'd be so proud of the way you've raised that daughter of yours."

My voice caught in my throat. "Mom."

"I know you'll never admit it, but part of you holding back on love again is because you haven't caught him yet." When I didn't answer, she added, "Am I right?"

"Please drop it," I pleaded. I didn't want to do this right now. The day had kicked my ass, my emotions were all over the place, too close to the surface. I felt raw.

What I wanted most right now, was to finish my drink while watching *SportsCenter*, jump in the shower, then go to bed for some much-needed sleep.

It's just too damn bad that we don't always get what we want.

*four*

Shane

I WOKE up feeling more exhausted than when I went to bed.

My dreams were filled with horrific scenes of the past. Laying there awake, I focused on the svelte blonde woman from across the street. Those liquid clear blue eyes, her slender figure, and that Cupid's bow mouth of hers; and don't get me started on the delightful way she'd blushed earlier. The way her skin pinked up, slowly spreading toward her neckline made me wonder how far the change of color had spread beneath the edge of that t-shirt of hers. Somehow, with thoughts of Emberlyn Roth, I was able to chase the nastiness of the last eight years away, enough to fall asleep again.

Then it would start all over.

During my shower, I made a point to look into my neighbor right away. Leaving the bathroom, towel tucked around my hips, I grabbed my cell and pulled up my contact list, hitting *call* when I found the one person I needed.

"Matthews, here."

Brycen and I had worked a few cases together, whenever I had time to moonlight for Nightshade Securities, a mutual friend's—Dalton Kippers'—company. If I didn't have a job on with the JPD, I'd probably be working with Kippers and his crew fulltime—something Dalton had been hinting about as of late.

"Bryce, I need you to look someone up for me," I tell him. "Name's Emberlyn Roth. Address..." I rattled off the information as well as what I knew about her.

"Seems like a quick and easy thing. By the address you gave me, isn't she one of your neighbors? What do you need this for?"

"Yeah." I sighed. "Rosie's been spending lots of time with her."

"Ah, got it," he said. "I'll have a file sent to your NSI email before the day's up, bro. Any chance you'll make NSI your permanent home any time soon?"

*Maybe.* I thought, but said, "Appreciated. I need to see this case through before even thinking on what Dalton's proposing."

"Right. I'll just leave your email active. You've been working with us often enough I doubt the big man will be opposed."

"Sure, you're just too lazy to be bothered with reactivating accounts," I razzed him. "Anyway, get back to me with what you find."

Before I could hang up, I heard Brycen's whispered, "Holy shit!"

"What?"

"Is she for real?" the guy asked.

"What do you mean?"

"She looks like *that*?"

"If you mean a tall blonde bombshell with—"

"With fuck me eyes, I—"

Something akin to possessiveness struck me. "Shut the fuck up!" I ordered.

Chuckling, Brycen said, "Relax man, but damn!"

I rolled my eyes. "Yeah, yeah."

"I'll get her details to you like I promised; but do me a favor?"

I sighed. "And what would that be?"

"If she's clean, promise me you'll give her a go."

"Bryce—" The man cut me off by hanging up.

What was up with people and their matchmaking these days?

As I left for work, I couldn't help but notice Emberlyn crouched down on her porch, picking some little box up. I'm not sure why I sat there for as long as I did, and I sure as hell didn't like the way her face paled to that of a white sheet when she looked inside the parcel. Looking around, she retreated to the safety of her home, then closed the door.

After witnessing this reaction of hers two days running, it was safe to say that her behavior set me on edge.

I assured myself that with Brycen looking into her past, I didn't need to worry about the unsettled feeling in my gut just yet, so I pushed it back, concentrating on the fucked-up day I knew I was about to have.

Not for the first time, the medical examiner, or ME, came back with his report; one that gave us absolutely nothing.

None of the fibers found on the body, during their preliminary sweep, were foreign. There were no hair, saliva, or skin follicles to speak of that belonged to anyone other than our latest victim, or her boyfriend, found on her body; yet there was clear indication that she'd had sexual penetration fairly recently.

Going over the evidence so many times made my head hurt, and I was sure Will felt the same way by how he seemed to be obsessively massaging his temples.

When my desk phone rang, I was glad for the reprieve. The call display announced my mother calling.

"Hey, Mom. How's—"

"Is Rosie with you?" The panic in her voice had me jumping to my feet.

I looked at my watch, my brows furrowing. "She's not back from school yet?"

"She should have been here half an hour ago," she said.

"Did you call the school?"

"They said one of their teachers saw her leave." She sniffled. "Shane, she's always home by now. *Always!*"

"I'm on my way." Hanging up on her, I headed for the door. "Rosie's missing."

"Need backup?" Will asked.

"I need you to go to the school and find out who saw what," I told him. "I'm gonna hit my neighborhood and see if anyone knows anything. The school's a five-minute walk for her, someone has to have seen something."

Packing up a few files, I rushed to my Escalade, cranked it, and headed home.

# *five*



IT WAS HAPPENING AGAIN—JUST like before I'd sold my previous home on the outskirts of Jacksonville when my divorce had been finalized.

The gifts. The mementos. The notes.

I thought I'd been rid of those when *he* went to jail. That's when Trevor Sykes should have ceased to exist for me. Or what I would have liked to have had happen.

I guess I didn't get my wish.

It petrified me that the man had found me after I'd put so much effort in keeping a low profile; but the man had always had his ways. Apparently, he hadn't lost those all-too important contacts of his while being locked-up for the last three years.

Some of the gifts were like those he used to get for me—his sick way of apologizing after terrorizing me—and others were odd and not what I'd have thought he would ever have thought to send. Those creeped me out the most.

When I moved to Jacksonville—my grandmother's former home specifically—I'd made sure that my restraining order encompassed a no-contact clause. I had one for the entire state of North Carolina. And I renewed it religiously, every year on the year.

The burning question in my mind, however, was why hadn't my lawyer contacted me about him being let out? He shouldn't have been eligible for parole for another six months.

"Unless he's got someone doing it for him," I thought aloud, sipping my cup of tepid coffee as I stared at the small white box I'd discovered on my front steps, just moments ago. The thing sat haphazardly on the kitchen island's edge.

Regardless, the whole thing was giving me the willies. What's more was the fact that my home now felt uncomfortable.

I no longer felt safe.

*Shane's a cop.*

Maybe I could mention what's been going on to him, or maybe I could just get him to give me a few leads on a decent security company to install a system in this place. Either way, knowing he was there—across the street—appeased my mind somewhat.

Setting my coffee down, I grabbed my latest eerie gift and made for the garage. I hadn't even stored the large bin up on its original shelf after I'd added yesterday's delivery to it. Lifting its lid, I dropped the tiny box to join the other, snapped the top back on, then hefted it back in its intended place. One I hoped to God and all things holy, that I'd never have to fetch again.

"Where were you?" I heard the little girl ask me when I walked into my little cottage.

I'd decided to work on invoices, and tagging product I hadn't yet packaged for the day and hadn't touched the production side of things. It just so happened I had left a few boxes that were to be delivered tomorrow in my little craft den, when I stumbled upon the little girl.

I jumped, clutching at my chest. "Rosie, you scared me half to death!"

She had the contrite look down pat, pout included. "I'm sorry, but I was so excited that you said we'd make some lip gloss together, I couldn't wait any longer."

This had me smiling, despite my heart breaking. I felt for the little girl, having lost her mother, and never really having a relationship with her. She looked up to me. She genuinely enjoyed my company—and I did hers—so I really didn't mind her regular interruptions. They broke up my day and served as a reminder that there was more to life than just work.

"You're right." I bit my lip. "Tell you what...How about we get together tomorrow? I never got around to picking up my supplies today, so I don't have some of the ingredients to make our lip glosses just yet." The disappointment in her eyes cut me to the quick. "But tomorrow, I'll have so much more, I'll even show you how to make your very own lotion. How does that sound?"

I swear she beamed from head to toe. "Really? My very own lotion?"

I nodded, unable to keep my smile at bay. She reminded me so much of myself at her age, when my grandmother had done the same thing with me. "Really. You'll have to come up with a name for it too, because I've never made lotion for little girls before."

"Can it be cotton candy like the gloss?"

I crouched down to where she was sitting and cupped her cheek. "I think that's a wonderful idea. Maybe you can help me figure out other things little girls like and we can create an entire line."

"For real?"

As soon as I nodded, she jumped up on a squeal and into my arms. The scent of her strawberry shampoo filled my nostrils, and I curled into her a bit more. She was such a precious character.

Pulling back, I noticed her school bag right next to where she'd been sitting. "Lana Rose," Her nose scrunched up, it was comical. I remained serious, however. "Why is your bookbag with you?"

"Because I came here right after school," she mumbled to her shoes.

"Does anyone know you're here?"

She hesitated before shaking her head to indicate the negative. "Nuh-uh."

"Rosie!" I scolded. "You can't do that, honey. Your grams and daddy are going to be worried."

Tears filled her eyes. "Am I in trouble?"

"Tell you what..." I grabbed her bag, throwing it over my shoulder, then grabbed her hand. "I'll talk to your grams and smooth things over. I'm sure she'll understand that you were excited." Pulling her toward the cottage's door, taking the time to lock it, I led us toward her home.

It wasn't Grams that opened however, it was Shane.

A very pissed off Shane.

"Daddy!" Rosie seemed to completely miss the fact that her father was staring at me with daggers.

"Go inside, princess. I need to have a talk with Emberlyn," he ground out.

*Uh oh!*

"But, Daddy—"

"Not now."

"It's my fault," she confessed. "I went to Ember's so we could make lip gloss, but she doesn't have the stuff, so I'll go back tomorrow, and—"

"Slow down, baby girl." He crouched down to her level. "Haven't we talked about this? You're supposed to come straight home from school, young lady."

"But—"

"We'll talk later, Rosie. Now go inside and help Grams."

"Yes, Daddy." She pouted. Looking back at me, she smiled guiltily. "I'm sorry I got us in trouble, Ember."

"No harm done, honey." I smiled for reassurance. "Thanks for visiting."

When the little girl disappeared, Shane stepped out onto the front porch, his intimidating stance making me take a step back, as he closed the door behind him.

"Listen—"

He lifted his hand to cut me off. "Thank you for bringing her back, but it doesn't excuse the fact that she's been with you for well on two hours." He was furious, as he should be. I didn't know the first thing about being a parent, but I suspected worry could sometimes bring out the worst in us. It seemed to be doing that to Shane right then.

"I—I didn't know she was there," I told him.

His eyes rounded in surprise. "*What?*" he hollered. "How does a grown-assed woman not know when a kid is around? Are you that self-absorbed that all you care about is your business?"

That got my back up in a hurry. So I made my advance. "Now wait a fucking minute, you jerk!" I poked him in the chest. "I work from home, and my business is based in that cottage out back, but it doesn't mean I spend my days there every day. I was working from the house today; invoicing, if you must know," I huffed. The gall of the man! "Why the hell am I telling you this anyway?"

"Ember—"

"She went straight to the cottage and waited there for me," I told him. "I figured out that she'd come to see me, instead of going home first, because I noticed her bookbag. If I hadn't needed those boxes, she'd still be sitting there."

"I—"

Emphasising my point with another poke, I added, "It's because of me that she's here right now, and you're not out there worried sick and still searching for her. So fuck you for insinuating that I had concocted some elaborate plan to kidnap or hold your daughter captive. I promise, next time she stops by, I'll send her right back. You have my word on that."

Without waiting for his reply, I turned on my heel and stormed off, crossed the street, and headed up my front steps. After unlocking the front door, I entered my home, slammed the fucking thing, and turned the deadbolt.

*Fuck him! Fuck men! Fuck them all!*

*six*

SHANE

I WATCHED Emberlyn's hips swing from side to side as she sauntered-stomped back to her house, thinking that not even Eva would have stood up to me like that. It brought a smile to my face; the first one of the day as a matter of fact.

The reality that I would have to reiterate the house rules, and discipline my daughter, had me quickly filling with dread. Being a parent sucked ass when it came down to making sure your kid toed the line. I'd much have rather had a playdate at the park.

Turning to enter the house, I found Rosie curled up on Mom's lap, sobbing into her chest. Mom gave me a sympathetic look, her eyes pleading me to go easy on her.

"Lana Rose, come here," I demanded softly.

She shook her head, burrowing further into my mother. "Please don't take her away. I don't want to lose Ember. She's my friend. She's fun. Don't make her go away, Daddy."

My heart broke because she thought that of me. "Why would you think that, honey?" Crouching down to her level, I lifted a hand to push back the strands of hair that had fallen from her ponytail.

"You're the police," she said simply, turning to look me in the eye with an incredulous expression. "You make the bad people go away. Ember wasn't bad. I was. She doesn't deserve it if you make her go away."

I gave her a sad smile. "Baby girl, I'm not going to make Ember go away." I paused to weigh my next words carefully. "But we are going to talk about the rules again, okay?" She nodded, settling her head on my mother's shoulder. "What's the first thing we do when we leave school?"

"Go straight home," she said. "But, Daddy, I was just so—"

"I know you were excited, Rosie. I understand that, but I need you to understand that you have people who will worry that something bad happened, if you don't do as you promised," I explained.

She bit her bottom lip, stopping it from its quivering. "I promise I won't do it again, Daddy."

Leaning forward, kissing the side of her forehead, I whispered, "That's good enough for me. Don't scare me and your grams like that again, please."

"I won't."

"Good." I smiled, gifted with one in return from my girl. "Now go get cleaned up for dinner."

"Okay." She jumped off Mom's lap and made her getaway. Pausing at the hallway entrance, she turned to me. "Daddy?"

"Hmm?"

She seemed to think about what to say, as if she wasn't sure she should say it at all.

"What is it, Rosie? You can tell me anything."

"You should maybe say you're sorry to Ember." With that, she was out of the room and out of earshot.

Mom spoke next. "She's right. You were a little harsh on her, dear."

I had been.

I guess I'll have to rectify that and soon.

Once Rosie was in bed, and Mom was engrossed in one of her favorite programs, I snuck out of the house.

Brycen had sent me all the information he could gather on Emberlyn.

I'd spent the better part of the evening digesting what I'd read, wondering, what with her past, how she'd managed to stand up to me as she had. It didn't take a genius to know I was an imposing man, but with what she'd been through, I sure as hell wouldn't have expected her to hold her own.

Suffice to say, I felt like a total asshole.

My knuckle met the wood of her front door, rapping on it three times.

I attempted it twice more before she finally opened.

"Listen, when someone doesn't open after your first knock, and they're home, it usually means that they don't want to see you," she snapped, crossing her arms over her chest. "Now, if you don't mind, I'd like for you to leave."

"I'm sorry," I uttered. "I overreacted, said a bunch of shit I didn't mean. You didn't deserve that."

"I didn't deserve a lot of things." She huffed away the loose strand of hair that had fallen across her face due to the night's breeze. "But it doesn't mean I didn't end up with it either. Apology accepted. Now get lost."

She went to slam the door in my face, but I stuck a booted foot out to block its progress.

"Come to dinner tomorrow night," I blurted without thinking.

That got me a wide-eyed look. "Are you out of your mind?"

"Let me make it up to you," I told her. "I know one little girl who'd love to know she hasn't lost a friend because her dad reached a new level of jackassery." She seemed to ponder my words, so I pushed further. "Please?"

"On one condition," she said.

"Uh…" I didn't know what to say to that.

"Rosie gets to come over tomorrow. I promised her we'd make her lip gloss today, but I never went to pick up some of the ingredients I needed for it, so I said we'd get together tomorrow," she explained.

"That's it?"

"That's it."

"I have no problem with that." Her lips stayed in a firm line at my words, but her eyes shined with pure joy. Fuck, I liked that look on her. Probably more than I should.

Looking down at my foot, I clued in that she was silently asking me to pull it back.

"What time's dinner?" she asked, the defensiveness gone from her voice.

"Is six okay, or am I taking you and Rosie away from your project?" I smirked.

She smiled. "No, six should be fine."

"See you then," I replied.

"Goodnight, Shane." Without waiting for my response, she shut me out, the sound of a lock engaging lending to our conversation's finality.

Sass.

The woman had plenty.

And I was a fan.

"Goodnight," I said to her door, chuckling as I turned to head back home.

# *seven*

EMBERLYN

CLOSING THE DOOR ON SHANE, I leaned back onto the surface and slumped down to the floor.

Dinner with Shane and his family?

I wasn't quite sure why I agreed. The man's preconceived notions about my character had been mean and unwarranted. If it hadn't been for the way he apologized, I would have dismissed him entirely. I wasn't a doormat. I wasn't weak, and I never would be again.

*I should have told him about those deliveries.*

It hadn't occurred to me, until everything had been said and done with Rosie, and then Shane's judgment, that the little girl shouldn't have been able to get inside my cottage.

With everything I'd been through thus far in my life, I locked everything. Everything! I was overly obsessive about it, to be honest. My house, my cottage, my car. Hell, I have double locks for the first two. It didn't matter that I was going to the curb to fetch my mail. I locked my doors and windows. It didn't matter if I was still inside my car. The doors were locked then, too.

So how was it that Rosie was able to get in?

The answer was simple.

Someone had been in there before her. It had to be it.

I shivered at the thought that my home—my sanctuary and workplace—had been invaded. The fact that an innocent child could have been harmed, by showing up like she had, brought a whole new slew of goosebumps. I felt violated.

Picking myself up off the floor, I made sure to check the door's locks, as well as all the windows and additional doors, before making my way to my bedroom, locking that door too.

Morning came too soon for me.

Last night, I'd slept with my bedside lamp turned on, and my Glock 26 under my pillow.

Every noise had me jumping, no matter how familiar the sounds were.

I'd lost count at how many times I reached for my gun whenever a twig snapped, or a vehicle came barreling down the street. A car door slamming had me bracing.

By three a.m., I'd resolved to talk to Shane about that security system I'd been debating—and dismissed all too easily— yesterday.

By lunchtime, I was coming out of my skin.

I felt like I was being watched, and it was proving a big distraction, if my nearly avoiding being run over by a black Chevy Avalanche was anything to go by.

Opting to stay where people were, I walked into Fairfax—a place I'd only heard of and hadn't been to before now—and ordered myself a burger with everything and their signature seasoned fries with a zesty cheese dip. It wasn't one of the healthiest options, but it was what I needed.

I was digging into my meal when a shadow darkened my space.

"Is everything okay, ma'am?"

Looking, up and up and up, I was greeted by a handsome man with jet-black hair and a pair of dimples that set my motor running. His smile was congenial, his eyes friendly. I instantly found myself wanting to ask him to sit with me because he made me feel safer.

One glance at his wedding ring, however, had me re-evaluating my intention to follow through with my thoughts.

"Dalton," he introduced himself by sticking out his big mitt of a hand, which I took.

"Emberlyn." My smile was forced ,and I could tell he knew this, his assessing gaze going into overdrive.

"Hey, babe?"

The man turned, his megawatt smile shining through toward a beautiful, short pregnant lady heading in our direction.

"I thought you said you'd wait in the car," he said, wrapping his arm around her shoulders, not having much choice but to wrap hers around his back and cuddle into his side.

Looking up at Dalton, she wore a sheepish expression. "Had to use the facilities," she explained, then looked my way and smiled. "You'd think I'd be annoyed, but I never thought I'd be pregnant so I'm nursing all these little annoyances for all they're worth. I'm Devolin, by the way. Was my husband harassing you?"

"Not at all." This time, my smile came easier, feeling more genuine. "Emberlyn." I presented my hand once more. Looking around, I realized I couldn't have picked a busier place—even if I tried. "Are you waiting for food?"

"Yeah."

"You can sit with me, if you'd like," I told them.

Devolin jumped right on in. "So, Emberlyn, what do you do?"

I bit my lip, debating on what to tell these people. "Ever heard of Lavender Sky?"

Devolin's eyes widened. "I love their products! They're small from what I know."

I nodded, grinning. It looked like I had a fan. "I make them," I announced.

"Seriously?" Dalton looked impressed.

"Mm-hmm." I snuck a bite of one of my fries, washed it down with a large gulp of Pepsi, and asked. "And how about you two?"

"Dalton owns his own security company," Devolin said, "and I work for him."

My eyes flickered between the two. What were the odds? "What kind of security?"

"Investigations, and sometimes, some search and recovery," Dalton said. "Devolin is my lead expert when it comes to following someone's electronic footprint."

My mouth formed an 'O' in understanding. "So you're a hacker?"

"Po-tay-to...po-tah-to," she murmured with a devilish gleam in her eyes.

The conversation at hand gave me a segue into my recent dilemma.

"You wouldn't happen to know of any decent companies that install security alarms, do you?" I blurted, immediately feeling bad that I was willing to talk about this with mere strangers before mentioning it to the neighbor, whom I already had a rapport with, and incidentally was also a cop. In my defense, if I couldn't mention it to Shane, who better than a security expert?

Dalton's eyes narrowed. "Emberlyn, are you in trouble?"

"I—I just can't be too careful, you know?" Cue the forced smile. "With my business growing, and me living alone, I want to make sure my assets are safe."

Something in the way Dalton looked at me told me he

didn't quite believe my words. To evade his scrutiny, I chose to look over at his wife. She wore a very similar expression to her husband's.

"Dalton knows of a few people that do systems. I'm sure we can help, right, babe?" She looked toward her husband.

The man nodded, his attention being beckoned by someone behind the bar. Standing from his seat, he offered me another one of his kind smiles, and then pulled his wallet out. Fishing through it, he slid a business card over the table, and toward me. "Give me a call. We'll help you out."

I nodded. "Thank you, I will."

"It was nice meeting you," Devolin said cheerfully.

"Likewise." I smiled again. "Both of you."

Just as they'd appeared, they left, their meals in tow.

# *eight*



I WAS ABOUT to leave work for the day when I saw Dalton standing by my car.

"Hey, what's up?" I asked the man. It wasn't unusual to see him stop by the precinct, seeing as we'd sometimes work cases together, but something told me his mere presence today wasn't one of police matter per se.

"Met your woman earlier today."

My brows hit my hairline. I wasn't expecting that. "Care to repeat that?" I hadn't asked him or Brycen for that at all. Hell, all I wanted was to know more about the woman my daughter was beginning to spend so much time with.

*Damn Brycen and his big mouth.*

"You think I wouldn't know what my own men were up to when it's my company?"

"I didn't ask for anyone to follow her," I defended.

"Relax." The man clapped the side of my arm. "Dev and I were at Fairfax grabbing lunch when I saw her. She seemed spooked."

That was news, yet it wasn't. I recalled the haunted expression when I'd spotted her first thing this morning; and yesterday for that matter. "What makes you say that?"

"She was barely eating. Her eyes were everywhere in the place. She tried to hide the fact I'd scared her, when I asked her if everything was okay," he rattled off. "And the kicker...after I told her what kind of business I was in, she asked me if I knew of any decent security alarm companies."

My body stiffened. "She what?" I couldn't blame her for being spooked, what with her history, but it surprised me that she felt so unsafe she'd feel the need for a security system.

The man nodded. "I'm going to recommend Stan. He did a great job with Devolin's system. He'll most likely give her a discount for having two places done at once."

I nodded. "Thanks."

"No prob." He stared me down. "Any breaks in this case of yours?"

"I still think it's *him*," I told Dalton. The team at Nightshade Security knew of my one and only suspect. I just hadn't imparted my suspicions to my partner, my boss, or the FBI, yet.

"Yeah, but you're not going to walk into that precinct and start pointing your finger at the fucker, are you?"

"No, I'm not." I sighed. "He'll slip up eventually, and when he does, I'll get him." It killed me that there would most likely be another death on my hands before I could possibly discover something to nail the bastard.

"My offer still stands, bro." He grinned. "Decent hours. You'll be able to spend more time with that little doll of yours. Working with people you trust. You wouldn't be under the same set of rules as you are now with the JPD. You already know this since you've been helping us out for over a year now."

Didn't I know it. That's what half my problem was. The other was the fact that our local judicial system was flawed. It's like they were letting just about anyone become cops these days. It was easy enough to pass the law enforcement entrance exam, but when you burned bridges along the way at the academy—particularly those with your evaluators—let's just say you're not the kind of cop I would want to know, and even less, one I'd like to work with. That was the case with an officer I'd had the displeasure of training nearly ten years ago. Casen Dodge.

Casen had been a self-entitled little shit. His father, a captain on the JPD, had made sure his son followed in their family's footsteps by greasing doorways to ease the passage. Unfortunately, due to my recommendations, Dodge didn't pass the academy. He'd moved away, yet, eight years ago, he'd also made a reappearance in Jacksonville, and dear old dad hired him on the force.

Despite my and other officers' grievances, we'd stayed stuck with him. He was nothing but a traffic cop with a grudge to hold.

And the only suspect in my wife's murder, not to mention the other fifteen that followed, even if I had yet to find shit to pin him with.

"You're right," I told Dalton. "I've been sick of the bureaucracy, for a while now; maybe I do need a change."

"Then let me know when you're ready. I could really use you on the team full time," he said. "Then again, you already know this since I've been trying to poach you for nearly a year now... ever since our case in Mexico with Devolin's uncle. Meanwhile, if you or your woman—"

I held my hand up. "D, she's not my woman."

The man smirked, and I wanted to wipe that look off his face. "Yet," he taunted.

Shaking my head, I hit the fob on my car to disarm its alarm. "I've got to get home. It's my night to cook and Emberlyn's coming over."

That warranted a chuckle from my friend. "You say she's not your woman, yet you're cooking for her. Could have fooled me."

"Let's just say she's coming over as my way of apologizing for being an ass to her last night."

He laughed at that. "Rough start, if you're not seeing one another, and you've already stepped in it." Humor left his features, replaced by an intense look that was sobering. "I saw what Bryce dug up on her."

"She's been through a lot," I mumbled. "I need to talk to her, especially since Rosie has been spending time with her more often lately. If there's trouble blowing back onto her, I can't let my girl get closer."

The man moved aside, nodding in agreement. "Enjoy eating crow."

After settling into the driver's seat, I smirked at the man. "You know what, I think I will." Slamming the door shut, I started the engine and put my car in drive.

Dinner was in the oven, Mom refused to relax and not contribute, so I set her on a salad. She was finishing up with that in the kitchen, Lana Rose talking to her about the basket of goodies she'd come home from our neighbor's with earlier. I was reviewing some of my case files.

Emberlyn came knocking at six o'clock on the nose.

My daughter exploded like a shot out of the kitchen and made a beeline for the front door before I could get there myself. When I did, however, I liked what I saw. A whole hell of a lot.

She wore a baby blue sundress with capped sleeves, her hair in a loose knot at the back of her neck. Her gray eyes seemed to have changed to match the shade of her attire. She didn't wear much makeup, but I could tell she'd put some effort into her look, right along with the dark red lipstick. My mind short-circuited as it began to envision how those red lips would look wrapped around my cock. As my eyes trailed lower, I became increasingly aware she was the perfect height for me.

Visions of me pushing her up against a wall, and taking her from behind, so I could grab her ample hips...

*Fuck, Brycen! Why'd you have to talk about her like—*

"Shane?" I heard Emberlyn's voice. She presented me with a bottle of wine. "I didn't want to come empty-handed."

"I said I was making dinner. That includes providing the drinks too." My voice was hoarse.

She shrugged. "Save it for some other time, if it doesn't go with what you have planned."

"Can I show you my room now?" Rosie interrupted.

Emberlyn's eyes searched mine for permission, which I granted with a nod of my head before I looked down at my girl. "Do it quick, honey. Dinner's ready."

"Okay!" Then she proceeded to pull Emberlyn along behind her, the woman still looking back at me.

By the time the two were out of the room, and I was standing there by myself, I knew I was in trouble.

# *nine*



DAMN, *he looks hot!*

I took a moment to cool myself down by inhaling deeply and exhaling slowly. A lot of good that did me when I inhaled the subtle spice mixed with a woodsy scent, and my nonexistent libido kicked in at a low purr.

*Get a hold of yourself! You're standing in his little girl's room!*

Making a great effort, I focused on all the pinks and purples surrounding me in the form of pillows, ruffles, paint, and other assorted accessories. It was cute. It was girlie. It was entirely Lana Rose.

"You've got a beautiful room, sweets," I told her.

The sight of a framed photo on the nightstand, of a woman holding a newborn baby, had me smiling—despite the sinking feeling in the pit of my stomach.

"That's my mom," Rosie explained. "Isn't she pretty?" She grabbed the frame and hugged it to her chest before handing it to me. "Daddy says I look a lot like her." Her smile made the entire room that much brighter. "Daddy told me she was the prettiest woman in the world."

My eyes were fused on mother and daughter, settled in a rocking chair, and a pang of sadness hit me. My butt found the edge of the little girl's mattress.

I could have had that once.

Clearing the emotion from my throat, I looked up at the little girl who stood in front of me expectantly and declared, "She's very beautiful, Rosie, but I think you're even more so."

She shrugged off my comment but gave me another one of her megawatt smiles. "Come on! We don't want to make Grams and Daddy wait." Rosie grabbed the frame from my hands and carefully set it back where it had been, before turning to me with a scrunched-up nose. "They get pissy when I take too long."

I giggled at that, even though I was sure that *pissy* was most likely a word she shouldn't be uttering at her young age. Getting up, I extended my hand to her. "Let's go, sweets."


Dinner was a quiet affair, entailing mostly of Rosie regaling her grams and father with what we'd been up to at my shop earlier today. Shane's mother seemed thoroughly interested in what her granddaughter had to say, yet the man himself, seemed more interested in watching me eat. It was a little disconcerting.

By the time dessert rolled around, Rosie offered to help her grams to plate everything, while Shane gave me a tour of their home.

We'd ended the main floor's tour in the den, but to be honest, I was too busy dealing with the fluttering sensation in my stomach, or recuperating from his slight touch to my lower back as he led me around, to really take in the beauty of the house.

"Thank you for coming over tonight," he said. "I have to admit I had an ulterior motive, aside from adding on to my apology."

"Forgiven," I croaked out.

The man's gaze was intense. "Is everything alright?"

"Why wouldn't it be?" I asked him.

"You seemed a little tweaked this morning. I saw you on your front step."

He made to approach me, which caused me to back up, right into the side of his desk, knocking a slew of papers and the file they'd been tucked into on the floor.

"Shit!"

Hurrying to my knees, I started rallying everything up in a pile when I felt Shane kneeling next to me.

"Let me. You shouldn't—"

I took a closer look at the shots of random pieces and froze, studying them.

"What? What is it?" he asked. "Do those look familiar?"

"They just remind me of something I once wanted to try and never have," I told him. "A photographic mosaic."

His body went rigid. "A what?"

"A photographic mosaic...or photomosaic," I explained. "It's when you take different images of the same size and compile them together to make a larger picture. Kind of like a puzzle, because each image has to be in the right color scheme to make the larger image true."

"You're shitting me, right?" he asked.

"Well, no," I said, then inquired further. "How many pieces do you have?"

He shrugged his shoulders. "I'd have to pull my files for the last eight years to know for sure. Do you know how to do these photo..."

"Mosaics?" I supplied. He nodded. "I've been wanting to try. Most people do these on computers these days, but I've seen them done by hand in a few galleries I've visited since I moved here." I studied the photos closer, then moved to inspect the next one in the pile in my hands, and gasped, dropping everything I held onto the floor.

"Emberlyn," I heard Shane say, but I was too busy processing the shock of what I saw. "Ember," he tried again.

"Shane! Ember! Dessert's ready!" Nora called out, but I couldn't respond, closing my eyes to try and imagine something beautiful to replace the horror I'd just seen.

"Give us a minute, Mom. We'll be right in." I felt his hand grab my chin, gently tilting my head until we were face-to-face. "Look at me, Emberlyn. Look at me right now!"

That worked.

My eyes snapped open, and I realized I wasn't breathing; the dark spots slowly clouded my peripheral vision, and my body swayed.

"Breathe, sweetheart. Breathe with me." Shane put a hand of mine on his chest, covering it with one of his as his other remained at my chin.

"T—that's the woman..." I swallowed the bile in my throat. "She was found dead in...Oh God!"

"Don't talk. Just breathe, baby."

Something in me snapped, and my body jerked back as if he'd hit me. Cold dread filled me along with even chillier memories. "Don't call me that!"

Shane's grip on me retracted as if I'd touched him with a cattle prod. "I'm sorry."

"Don't call me that," I repeated at a whisper. "It's what he used to call me."

"Who?"

That's when I realized I'd said too much.

Jumping to my feet, I backed toward the front of the house, stuttering, "I—I have to go."

"Wait!"

I shook my head, swallowing what I knew would be my dinner coming up to greet me again. I didn't want to be here when it did. "I'm sorry. Tell your mom and Rosie thank you."

Turning, I rushed out of the Peters' residence as if my hair was on fire, barely making it to my front bushes before my stomach revolted, turning the wonderful dinner that Shane had put together into plant fertilizer.

What I didn't expect were the steel bands that would come to wrap around me while I sobbed and dry-heaved.

# *ten*



"IS EVERYTHING OKAY?" Mom had run into the den as soon as the front door slammed shut. "What happened? Where's Ember?"

I shook my head. "I've got to go after her." I couldn't explain because I didn't really know the whole of it myself. "Can you look after Rosie? And don't let her come in here. I'll clean this up when I get back."

She nodded, a distraught expression entering her gaze as she peered at the mess around me. "Okay, baby," she choked.

I winced. "Mom—"

"Go," she said. "You need to go. I'll go check on Rosie."

Nodding, I hurried out the front door, catching sight of Emberlyn hunched over one of her bushes, her back and shoulders heaving violently.

*Fuck!*

I didn't hesitate. Rushing to her, I wrapped my arms around her middle and held on to the sobbing woman, who in turn began to scream like a banshee.

"Let me go! Help! Someone—"

My hand snapped up to cover her mouth, and I bent my head to the bucking woman's ear. "Shh," I whispered as she continued to fight me. I got a kick in the shin, causing me to groan. "It's Shane, Ember. It's me. I'm here."

Her body went slack, but shock set in almost immediately and she began shaking like a leaf, her sobs resuming.

"Let's get you inside, sweetheart."

She didn't argue. In fact, she didn't say anything or physically acknowledge me.

Bending down to pick up the tiny purse she'd dropped to the ground, along with her keys, I made to pick her up in my arms.

"I—I can walk," she said, teeth chattering.

"Okay," I said softly. "How 'bout you hold onto me, and we'll take it slow. I'm not liking your color right now."

I didn't realize how extreme her fear was until I'd closed the door behind us, and attempted to usher the woman toward where I knew the living room would be, but she shrieked, "Lock the door!"

After that task was done, we made our way to the couch.

Emberlyn quickly backed into the armrest, curling her knees up to her chin. I grabbed the throw off the back of the sectional and draped it over her.

"Let's get you a glass of water," I told her, heading toward the kitchen.

In case you were wondering, this wasn't my first time inside this house. I'd been here plenty while growing up, but it sure had changed. Emberlyn had put her mark on her grandmother's old place, and it was a warm and pleasant one with a more modern flare to it. I approved.

Glass in hand, I set to run the water until it was nice and cold, filling it from the tap.

When the floor creaked beneath my feet on my return,

Emberlyn jumped, panic in her eyes until they settled on me. She melted into the cushions almost immediately with palpable relief.

She didn't waste time, grabbing the glass from my hands, chugging its contents immediately. I took the glass from her and settled it atop the one coaster I saw on the coffee table before crouching down in front of her.

"Better?" I asked. She nodded. "Want to talk about it?" She shook her head, no. "Do you want me to leave?" Another shake. This had me standing to sit next to her, but not too close, since I didn't want to make her more uncomfortable than she clearly was.

That plan was squashed as soon as my ass met the cushion and she launched herself at me.

"Whoa! Calm down, sweetheart. You're okay," I whispered my reassurance into the side of her face, one arm wrapped around her back, her legs over my lap, and the other sifting into her hair. I couldn't help myself. I pulled the pin that held her hair together, chucking the thing onto the coffee table, and resumed stroking her.

For a long moment, we sat together, neither of us saying a word, when so much remained to be said. Then she opened up.

"He used to call me b—baby," she told me what I already knew. "My husband...that's what he'd call me, when he tried to gain my forgiveness after he'd beat me." My blood began to simmer. "Trevor and I had a very volatile relationship. I would do everything he asked of me, and he'd never be happy. I learned to be subservient to him early on. Mouthing off only got me punished. So I did what I had to until I could get out. I just didn't do it fast enough."

"Sweetheart, I know," I said against her hair.

"You know?" she whispered, pulling back so she could look at me, then realization must have hit her. "You're a cop, of course you'd know."

"Detective." I smirked.

Her brown scrunched up. "Huh?"

"I'm a detective. I wouldn't know about your case, but since my girls have been spending time with you...I just hope you're not mad that I had someone look into you."

"No." She forced a smile, but it was nice seeing something other than tears in her stormy gray eyes, despite my apprehensiveness to her reaction that I might have overstepped my bounds with her past. "You have a daughter...a family to protect. I'd have done the same thing." Settling in against my front again, her hand came up to lay on my chest. "Thank you, Shane."

Swallowing the large lump in my throat, I rasped, "You're welcome."

Then silence enveloped us once more—not awkward—comfortable.


Something stirred me awake, but I wasn't quite sure what it was until I saw a blanket being draped over me.

"I'm awake," I husked.

"I'm sorry. We fell asleep, and—"

Grabbing her wrist to stay her movements, I did an ab curl to sit up. Emberlyn's free hand sifted into my hair. She was standing between my legs, looking down as she massaged my scalp. Fuck, it felt good. I closed my eyes to enjoy the intimacy of the moment. So much so that I gripped her hips.

"I should go," I whispered, my eyes opening to meet hers.

"Yeah."

"It's late."

"Uh-huh." Her head bobbed up and down with her words.

This made me smirk, and confess, "I don't want to leave you."

"Rosie'll need her father tomorrow morning," she rationalized.

"Fact, but it still doesn't make me want to go."

Her smile showed her pleasure at my words. "I'll be fine."

"You're sure?" I asked.

"Pinky swear. Go home, Shane. Your family needs you."

That had me smirking. "If you need me, you know where I'll be." I guided her back, so I could get up, curling my hands around the sides of her face, then tilted it forward so I could touch my lips to her forehead. "Walk me out?" When my feet hit her front steps, I gave her one last assessing gaze.

"I'll be fine." She laughed nervously. "Thanks again."

I smiled, then bent to kiss her cheek. "You're welcome again," I whispered, then left, but not before I heard the clicks of her front door locking.

# *eleven*

EMBERLYN

GETTING BACK to sleep after Shane left had been a tough feat, but one I'd finally managed at about four in the morning.

I woke up, feeling refreshed, albeit a little hot and bothered from the steamy dream I'd had about my neighbor: the single father.

Remembering last night's events, I cringed at the memory of my upchucking in my front bushes. How embarrassed I should be feeling that Shane—the object of my subconscious desire—had seen my stellar digestive pyrotechnics, but oddly enough, I felt no shame. Maybe it had been the way he'd been tender and understanding in the aftermath of my freak-out. Perhaps it was the way he actually listened to what I had to tell him about my past, taking my words in stride, digesting them. None of last night had me feeling regret. Quite the opposite really. I was feeling drawn to a man that I shouldn't even be contemplating anything with, but my libido just didn't quite get the memo. And my heart seemed to be following that same path. My head however...just wasn't willing to make that leap yet.

. . .

In need to clean up last night's mess, I slipped into a pair of yoga pants, a loose-fitting tank, and headed to the side of the house for the garden hose. I could only imagine the stench of old bile and partially digested food that awaited me. My stomach churned at the thought. When I got myself set up though, I noticed that everything had been cleaned up and my front gardens had been watered.

"It's the least I could do," made me jump, clutching at my chest as I whirled around to face Shane.

"You did this?"

He shrugged his shoulders, a bashful look covering his face.

Shane Peters, shy?

Confident, yes.

Potent, without a doubt.

But shy? I never thought I'd see the day!

"You didn't have to do that."

"I know, but I felt bad for being the cause of all of this." He motioned at the bushes with his arm. "I really didn't want you to deal with the memory of my stupidity."

I melted a little at his sweet intention. It had been a long time since someone had done something so small to take care of me. "It wasn't stupid," I whispered, looking at my hands.

"What's that?"

Looking up at him, I cleared my throat and repeated, "It wasn't stupid. It's sweet. Thoughtful. Thank you."

I giggled at the *aw, shucks ma'am* expression that spread over his face.

His eyes darkened. "I like that," he rumbled.

The sound froze in my throat as I croaked out, "What?"

"Your laugh." He smiled. "I've seen you smile. I've even seen you laugh at something Rosie's said." He shook his head. "But I've never *heard* you laugh or giggle. You should do it more often."

My mouth ran dry. Words evaded me.

Shane must have known I was beginning to feel a little uncomfortable, so he chose that moment to make his escape. "I should go. I have some errands to run before I'm due to take Rosie to dance class."

"Okay."

"I'll see you later?"

Figuring it was a given, considering we were neighbors, and his daughter was popping by later today, I simply nodded.

Later that Saturday morning, I got in touch with Dalton to get the information on the security system lead he had for me.

Call me surprised when Stan, the system expert, announced he had been expecting my call, and he'd be by after lunch if I was free.

I agreed straightaway.

After lunch, and right at one, Stan was standing on my doorstep.

It took him a couple of hours to devise a plan and work out a quote for me. His being thorough would keep me safe, but it would also cost me a pretty penny.

"I'm not sure I can afford this," I told Stan. "What if I go with the next lowest package, could I still have the sensor lights and everything else added on later?"

He gave a curt nod. "You could, but it'll cost you extra in the long run. I recommend getting everything done at once, that way there's less likely of a chance of glitches with the programming, so if your only issue is the cost, we can work something out."

Biting my bottom lip, I took another look at the comparison between what Stan was recommending and the step lower. There was a lot missing. I'd have to shuffle my funds around, and part of the expense could be written off when I filed my taxes. I shook off my internal rationalizing and smiled shyly at the man standing before me. "Can you give me a few days to think on it?" I asked.

Chuckling, he returned my smile. "That's fine. I'm sure my wife will thank you for returning me to her torture. She's been wanting me to paint the baby's room. I suppose I've put it off for long enough."

My smile got wider at the man's evident excitement despite his words. "Congratulations."

"I'll leave these brochures and the quote with you." Stan handed me the pocket folder containing everything. "Call me anytime, day or night, if you have any questions," he said, as we walked toward the front door.

"I will," I promised.

When I opened the door, there stood Shane and Rosie.

"Good to see you, Shane."

The man looked between Stan and me. "Everything okay?"

I nodded, while Stan answered. "Just setting this pretty little thing up with a system."

Shane nodded. "How's Becky?"

"Itching to get that little terror out of her," Stan told him, both men laughing. "Gotta run. Now that I'm done here for the day, I'm going to give my wife the baby room of her dreams." Winking at Rosie, he headed for his truck.

# twelve

SHANE

"YOU KNOW STAN?"

Once the man had driven off, I turned to Emberlyn. "Yeah. He's one of the best when it comes to security systems. You chose well."

"He came highly recommended," she said. "I just need to look at my books and make sure I can afford it. I have a few extra orders this month, so I think I should be able to slide it."

Without thinking, I blurted, "If you need—"

"God no!" she exclaimed. "I'll be fine. It might be tight for a month or two, but I have a fail-safe."

"Okay." I watched her, watching me, that stubbornness lighting her eyes.

"Daddy, you can go now," Rosie cut in.

A humored expression replaced that of Emberlyn's one of stubbornness, and I watched as my neighbor tried to stifle the smile that was threatening to break out on her face at my daughter's words.

"What if I don't want to go?" I asked my little girl.

"Then you'll be making bubble bath and cream that stinks, but it makes your skin tingle," Rosie stated.

My lips quirked as I asked Emberlyn, "Stinky creams sell?"

She lost her battle with her smile and added a soft giggle to the mix. "It's stinky to her, because she's all for the berries and cotton candy." Rosie giggled when the woman flicked her nose. "It's stinky because I use arnica, St. John's wort, and eucalyptus in my pain salve. She was around after I'd finished making a batch of infused oils to see if I could bring in a massage oil component to the mix."

"Ah." Honestly, I'd heard about the healing properties of herbs before, but I've always relied on my trusty *BENGAY* to soothe away the aches and pains. The way the woman spoke of mixing everything, however, had me interested in discovering more about her knowledge.

*You shit! You want to know more than that and you know it.*

If I was being honest with myself, yeah, I did want to know what made Emberlyn tick.

"You all set?" The woman broke me out of my head as she put out her hand to my daughter.

"Uh-huh!"

"Are you staying?" she turned to me. "You're more than welcome to."

"You don't mind?"

"I might put you to work." She winked, a mischievous smirk playing at her lips.

"Then point me to my station, boss," I joked.


The contrast between the two females before me was startling. Emberlyn was the light to my daughter's darkness, but they fit.

I watched as the two worked side by side, stirring whatever that crap was the woman had set in front of me earlier, to mash up. Emberlyn's gentleness, compassion, and patience with my little girl had me feeling things that perhaps I shouldn't, but I couldn't help it.

I could see how one brought out the best in the other. Lana Rose had always been a happy little girl, but I'd noticed a change in her as of late. It's as if she was missing that motherly bond. She had my mother, but I knew it wasn't enough. It wasn't the same. In this moment, the reality hit harder than at any other point since I lost my wife. My Eva.

Despite this, I couldn't bring myself to get out there and date. I didn't want just anyone. I wanted *the* one. Eva could never be replaced, and I'd always love her. Having Emberlyn around, seeing how she and Rosie interacted, catching the jokes, the laughter...the smiles, I knew I'd found a gem in this woman. She made my daughter shine with happiness. She adored her, that much was evident, and when Rosie showed her any form of affection, the woman never hesitated, giving it back twofold.

*Why haven't I caught on until now?*

It showed that I'd been somewhat of an absentee father.

Shame filled me at that realization. Apparently, Emberlyn noticed too.

"You okay?" she asked, after Rosie had excused herself to use the bathroom.

"Yeah," I grumbled. "Are you two always like this?"

Beaming at me, she confessed, "Yeah. We usually talk more than today, though. I think it's because you're here." She took away the pot of liquid I was stirring, turning the hotplate off and moved the lot to the side.

Leaning forward, my chin in my hand, elbow on the counter, I returned her smile from across the counter. "So what do you ladies talk about?" I wiggled my brows.

She harrumphed. "Like I'd tell you," she teased. "It's girl code not to say anything."

Her eyes widened when I got to my feet, then came at her, our eyes never unlocking from their hold. Coming to a stop in front of her, I reached up to cup her cheek. "I like the way you are with her," I rasped.

"You've got a really great little girl, so it's easy. She's pretty amazing," she whispered.

"You've opened your door, *and* your heart to her, when you didn't have to," I stressed. "You're amazing." She blushed at my words. Her eyes showed me she felt so much more than I knew, and I wanted to discover those hidden thoughts. Those feelings. Just...everything. "Go out with me," I blurted in a whisper.

"We shouldn't." She swallowed hard, sadness evident in her words, the brightness in her eyes dimming. "It's not that I don't want to, Shane, it's—"

"Why not?"

"What if it doesn't work out?" Her gaze filled with sorrow. "Rosie loves coming here. It would break me to lose her, Shane."

The conviction in her words had me weighing my next ones carefully. "I would never take her away from you." As if a magnet was pulling us closer together, we each stepped toward the other. "I can see you two have a bond, but something's going on here, between us, and I feel it needs exploring. Can you deny it?"

Fire entered her gaze. "I can, if it's safest for that little girl."

Cupping her neck in my hands, I smirked, my eyes flicking to her lips. "Your body's telling me the truth, when this beautiful mouth of yours is spouting lies." My thumbs ran from the hinge of her jaw to stop on that plump lower lip of hers.

Her breath hitched. "I—I..." She licked her lips, the tip of her tongue brushing my digits.

Nuzzling her nose with mine, I said with absolute certainty, "You want this, sweetheart." I moved my hands back to the sides of her neck and very lightly brushed my lips against hers. "You want this as much as I do." She leaned in as if expecting a kiss, but I held back, watching the attraction swell in her eyes before I went in for the kill. "Stop lying to me...to yourself...and put us both out of our misery. Just say yes."

To prove my point further, I fused my mouth to hers, feeling her body shudder against mine as she gave in.

The creak of the bathroom door had Emberlyn stiffening, but I soothed her with a few gentle pecks before she let her forehead fall to my shoulder.

"I'll go out with you," she capitulated, shivering slightly as my hands rubbed up and down her back soothingly.

"Thank you, sweetheart." I kissed the top of her head, then made my way back to my seat, my smile feeling like a permanent fixture on my face.

"Persuasive jerk," she mumbled, but I didn't miss the smile she was also sporting on those deliciously kiss-swollen lips of hers. "Here." She pushed a mortar and pestle my way with more herbs in it. "Make yourself useful and use those muscles to mash more of this into a powder."

Suffice it to say, when Rosie returned, she entered a room filled with laughter.

Mine and Emberlyn's.

It fucking felt great.

# *thirteen*

THE DOORBELL RANG and my already frayed nerves got the better of me.

Running to get the door, I managed to somehow stub my toe on the leg of the table by the main entrance.

"Fuck!" I howled, followed by more cursing.

"Emberlyn, you okay?" Shane asked through the door.

"Shit. Fuck. Damn." I hopped on one foot, checking out my big toe, shocked to see that I'd done a good job of trying to kill it, by the blood seeping out from under the toenail. "I'll be right there."

Hobbling over the rest of the way, I unlocked the deadbolt, turned the knob, and swung the door inward.

What greeted me took my breath away.

*Damn!*

The man sure made my knees go weak. I had to brace myself on the entryway's framework. Or maybe that was because of my throbbing toe. I winced.

"What happened?" Shane pushed his way inside, closing the door behind him when he saw me favoring my left foot.

63

"Stubbed my toe," I mumbled.

"It's bleeding. Let's check it out." He lifted me up in his arms and headed toward the living room.

"Shane!" I squeaked, but I simply couldn't tell him to put me down. His gesture made me feel cherished and safe. Despite the numerous times I thought about canceling out on the man, *this*—his knight in shining armor complex that is—simply had me melting and craving more of what I'd never had. So instead of bailing on the man, like my head told me I should, I followed my heart. All right...my pussy too, even though there was no way I'd go that far on a first date.

As soon as my ass met the couch, Shane was on his knees, my foot in his lap as he produced a hanky—yes, the man apparently carried a hanky—from his back pocket and proceeded to dab at the blood while inspecting my injury. "I don't think we can know for sure without X-rays, but it looks like you could have broken it."

That was the last thing I wanted to hear, but despite the pain in my foot, I found myself breathing deeply to calm the fluttering butterflies that had taken residence in my stomach.

"I can't have a broken toe! I've got boxes to pack and shipments to deliver to my clients. I—" The fact that Shane's shoulders were shaking with laughter incensed me. "What's so funny?" I grumbled.

"What are the odds I would plan a night that entailed dancing, and this is what happens?" He grins up at me, his eyes displaying heat as he all of a sudden went completely serious. "And I don't dance."

That had me giggling. "Then why would you plan a date like that?"

"Because I found myself wanting to do that with you." Cue those fluttering butterflies! All hints of my earlier nerves were officially forgotten. "Now I'm thinking, let's get you checked out, come back here, and settle in for some pizza and a movie. How does that sound?"

My mouth was dry as the desert, but I managed to eke out an, "Okay." I wasn't much of a dancer anyway.

"A fucking fractured toe," I grumbled as Shane got into the driver's seat. "How many times does someone stub their big toe in a lifetime, and I have to be the one to end up the gimp?"

His laugh was quiet, as he set a hand on my thigh. "Look at it this way, if you structure your days right, I can help you with your deliveries." He winked, then took his hand back to start his car.

"That's highly inconvenient, Shane."

"It's just until you're able to do it on your own again, Emberlyn," he retorted.

I snorted. "Get me that pizza and take me home, will you?"

His rich timbered laugh boomed out. "Your wish is my desire."

I rolled my eyes at his dramatics.

*Those are huge words to live by, big man.*

When another boom of laughter hit the interior of the car, I knew I'd spoken my thoughts aloud.

"Shit," I muttered under my breath, pinching the bridge of my nose as I shook my head.

"I have no problems to live by them, sweetheart." Putting the vehicle in gear, he grabbed my hand and kissed the knuckles, a shiver coursing through my body as he twined our fingers together and kept hold.

"Hell," I mumbled, training my gaze through the passenger side window, my breath speeding up, my body heating. Something told me Shane Peters was a man of his word.

We'd demolished the pizza and had vetoed the movie, for the time being, in lieu of conversation. Normally, I was a closed book, but with Shane, I found it quite easy to open up to him. Of course, it could have been the bottle of wine we'd emptied. I was good. I was happy. I was feeling no pain at all.

Shane moved my legs so they draped over his lap, causing me to turn and lean my inner arm up on the couch backrest. I rested my head in my hand, my other one holding on loosely to my nearly empty glass of wine.

"So," he started, "lotions and potions, huh?"

My laugh was light. Relaxed. "Yeah, lotions and potions."

"How'd you get into it?"

"My grandmother taught me it was pointless to buy something when you can make it," I explained. "I took some of her recipes, dabbled with them, adding things here, taking out things there...Next thing I knew, I had friends wanting my stuff. One of them convinced me to go to smaller shops around Jacksonville and see if they'd be willing to sell my products."

His gaze was one of wonderment. "And the rest is history, right?"

I grinned. "Not exactly. That same friend stole from me. She put her own line of shit out with some of my recipes. I should have known to copyright them."

"I take it she's no longer a friend," he said rhetorically.

"No, she most certainly is not. Anyway, I ended up starting from scratch again, reinventing my brand, my products, and expanding from there." I couldn't hide my prideful smile. "Grandma passed not too long after that, and I moved in here."

"What about Trevor? Was he part of the reason why you relocated?" he asked.

I nodded, my nose scrunching up. I knew this topic of discussion would come to pass even though I'd much have preferred to bypass it altogether. "He's been in jail for three years now," I explained. "I put him in there with my book, and his brother helped me. I don't talk to Darren anymore. We figured it would be safer to part ways when the divorce was finalized."

By book, I meant something more along the lines of a binder

filled with photos and diary entries of each time my ex had hit me hard enough to leave a mark.

"I'm glad." His hand brushed the tendril of hair that dangled at my temple. "I read up on him too, by the way."

My smile was a sad one. "I figured you probably would after you looked me up."

"He's eligible for early parole," he said, stroking the side of my face. "I know you have a restraining order on him that covers the entire state, but have you given it any thought if he'd try to track you down?"

I hesitated. "It's why I'm having the security system put in," I whispered, unable to meet his eyes. We were having such a nice evening. I really didn't feel like ruining it by broaching the subject of my mystery packages and notes. Not yet anyway.

"Good," he said softly, his hand moving to just below my chin, tilting my face up. "I want you to know that I'm here."

"I know."

"No, Emberlyn." He licked his lips, then leaned in. "I'm here to help. I'm here to protect you. I'm here to—"

Leaning up the rest of the way, I snared his lips with mine.

God! The man couldn't be more perfect. He said all the right things.

This kiss was pure sweetness. It was a thank you. It was a capitulation. It was a statement that I wanted more of what was going on between us. Much more. Fuck the one date!

Licking the flavor of him off my lips before pecking his mouth one last time, I ran my nose up his and smiled sweetly. "How 'bout that movie?"

# *fourteen*



HERE WE WERE, lazing on the couch, Emberlyn at my side, but splayed mostly on top of me. We were maybe halfway through *Deadpool* when I whispered into the crown of her head. "I fucking missed this."

She lifted her head, studying me. "I take it you haven't dated much since..."

I shook my head. "Having a child to care for, and a crazy career as a detective, doesn't really leave me with much time. Then again, I haven't really felt the urge to make time and get to know someone beyond the superficial, until recently." My eyes bored into hers.

"You mean me?"

I grinned. Why was she so surprised? "You," I confirmed, waiting until she settled her head on my chest once more before I gave her more of myself. "I miss cuddling in front of the TV, quiet nights in, good conversation...good company. I miss having someone for myself that gives a damn about more than just themselves. Someone that can challenge me."

"I miss it too and I've never had it," she admitted at a whisper, squeezing my middle with the arm that was draped over it. "I want it though."

"You have it, sweetheart," I told her, pressing my mouth to her hair again. "For as long as you want it. With me."

She snickered. "You really know how to tempt a girl, you know that?"

"You make me want to tempt you," I confessed.

Arching back to look down on me again, both her hands came to rest on my chest as she made to center herself over me.

This position could potentially get us in hot water.

Leaning into me, her eyes played between mine and my mouth as she whispered, "I think all you need to do is breathe to do that."

That's when I lost my ability to think clearly.

With a hand at the back of her head, the other on her back, I guided her mouth to mine in a savage kiss.

The moment she moaned, I took the opportunity to thrust my tongue into her mouth and get a thorough taste of her.

Her body melted into mine.

Rolling us over was a little tricky, but with little urging on my part, Emberlyn followed my lead, and that's how I came to lay on top of her, my mouth releasing hers for the sake of exploration.

Lifting her leg to wrap around my waist had made the hem of her dress ride up, exposing the edge of her underwear. My hand traced the smoothness of her thigh, rubbing up until it found lace.

I paused by her collarbone, my forehead dropping there as I struggled to breathe. "She wears fucking lace."

"I like things that make me feel pretty," she panted. "You should check out the matching bra."

I reared back like a shot and stared at her shocked expression.

Seconds later, she covered her face, giggling into her hands. "I can't believe I just said that. It has to be the wine."

Chuckling, I pulled her hands down from her face, kissing her nose as I did it. "You can't tease me like that and expect me not to go looking." I waggled my brows, generating another laugh from her. "Fuck, I love that sound." I pressed my mouth to hers in a hard and all-too-brief kiss. "Your say, sweetheart. If you want to continue this, I'm not sure I can do it on the couch."

"Then take me to bed, Shane."

With my hands on her hips, my body pressed against the back of hers, Emberlyn led us to her bedroom.

By the time we reached her bedside, I bent my head to kiss her shoulder, toward the back of her neck, as I unzipped her dress.

"Are you sure?" I asked against the smooth skin of her shoulder. She nodded. "Sweetheart, I need to hear you say it."

"I'm sure, Shane."

To emphasize her point, she turned in my arms, and allowed the fabric to her blush-colored dress to drop to the floor. Furthermore, her hands made a grab for the buttons of my shirt, working each of them through their eyelets, before pushing the garment off my shoulders and down my arms.

"I'm glad I checked," I rasped, as she skimmed her hands over my chest, pressing her lips over my left pec in a tender kiss. "It only proves I was right. You can drive me crazy by simply wearing lace."

I felt the puff of air over my chest from her quiet laugh. "That's encouraging." Pulling back to meet my eyes, I was greeted with her mischievous smirk. "Now let's do something about those pants, Detective Peters."

The moment her dainty fingers snuck beneath the waistband of my pants, to undo the button and zipper, my brain short-circuited. Her eyes never once left mine as she shimmied the slacks over my hips and down my ass. Gravity took over the rest as I sifted my hands into the back of her blonde locks and brought my mouth down on hers.

The dazed expression on Emberlyn's face, when I pulled away, urged me forward.

Guiding her to sit, then lay back over her comforter, I paused, standing above her, admiring the sight sprawled before me.

"Exquisite," I stated, wrenching my feet from my pant legs, removing my socks in the process.

"You're looking pretty damn fine, yourself." She winked.

"Beautiful, smart, honest, sweet, and just the right amount of sass," I muttered, crawling up onto the bed, before lowering myself over her. "It's sexy as fuck."

Her heated gaze turned to one of softness. "Shut up and kiss me, Shane," she whispered, her voice holding a subtle quiver.

Her words had me grinning. "Any particular place you'd like my kisses?"

"You can start with my mouth." She cupped the side of my face. "I like your kisses. Anywhere else those lips touch will simply be a bonus."

# *fifteen*



OH. My. Sweet. Baby. Jesus!

The fact the small patch of lace covering my pussy, or the thin layers covering my tits, hadn't been incinerated yet, was shocking.

Shane had me writhing, simply by using his hands and mouth. His sinfully wicked mouth. The sucking, licking. The nipping. It was the most brilliant kind of torture I'd ever experienced, and I wanted to submit to his every whim.

I was staring down my body, at the head of mussed up dark blond hair that hovered just above my pelvis.

His gaze met mine. "My mouth is watering for a taste of you," he growled.

God, did I want him to do that. "Please." He had me in such a heated tizzy that I wasn't above begging at this point. It had been so long.

Shane reached for the sides of my underwear, my hands covering his, guiding their removal so I could maintain a sense of control.

The man's nostrils flared at the sight of my bare smooth

skin. I was thankful I'd made the time to see my usual aesthetician for my regular waxing appointment last week. My heat throbbed at Shane's blatant approval of my grooming choice.

Much to my joy, the man didn't waste time.

He wasn't gentle with me like I'd expected. Don't get me wrong, he wasn't rough either. He just had this kind of presence to him. Dominant. Sure. He knew what he wanted and wasn't afraid to get it. To take it. I normally shied away from people with dominant personalities, especially since Trevor, but Shane...there was just something about him. Maybe it was because he was a cop, but I just knew—down to the very fibers of my soul—that he would never deliberately harm me.

Shane's lips surrounded my clit, two fingers maniacally hitting that sweet spot inside me, I had no doubt I was done for. Seconds later, I found myself teetering over the edge of bliss.

"Shane, fuck!" I screamed as my orgasm rushed through me, my body bowed tight.

"Holy." He kissed my stomach. "Shit." His tongue licked a trail up my sternum. "That was hot." He nipped my jaw, then settled between my thighs, his cock nestled against the tender flesh he'd just worshipped with his mouth. "I'm gonna need another taste. But later."

"Mmm," was all I could muster. I was basking in the afterglow of Shane's sensational display of sexual prowess, and if I were being entirely honest, I couldn't think, let alone see straight, at that moment.

"Sweetheart?" His body shook with silent laughter. This made his very erect cock vibrate over my clit, reminding me of the ache that still lingered deep inside me, despite my orgasm.

Moaning at the sensation, I spread my legs further apart, and wrapped them around his hips, my feet nudging the cheeks of his ass forward. *God, you're such a slut.* I ignored my inner voice and pressed against Shane's ass again. "More."

"I need to get a condom," he confessed, running his nose the length of mine. "But if this thing between us continues, I want to feel you bare. I get tested every six months because of work. I'm clean and well..."

I pressed my mouth to his, assuaging his self-conscious rambling. I knew he wasn't a monk, but I also knew he didn't make time for himself often.

I'd never had a man bare before. Not even my ex-husband. "I'm protected," I told him. "And I'm clean too."

His eyes darkened at my words. He then proceeded to coat his cock with my juices, sliding it through my pussy lips, making me wetter with each pass. His gaze never left mine.

"Shane," I pleaded, pulling him closer with my legs.

He pushed his tip in enough to tease me, his head falling forward to rest on my collarbone. With just the tip, I got a real sense of how large he was.

"Fuck!" He didn't push in any further, or pull out, so I encouraged him with another nudge of my legs, a hiss escaping his lips. "So tight. So hot..."

"Take me." I was desperate, my arms rounding his shoulders. "Suit up if you have to, then take me. *Please!*"

His head lifted, his mouth came to mine with a tender kiss, then he pulled back as his hips moved forward, slowly filling me.

I can't tell you how erotic it was to look into someone's eyes as he possessed you in the most intimate of ways, because there were no words for it.

Leaning onto his elbows, his hands delved into my hair, Shane's eyes remained fused to mine, our lips touching, yet not kissing...simply breathing each other in.

"You're fucking perfect," he whispered, his girth stretching me with a sweet pain, burying himself as far as he could go.

Pulling out slightly, he plunged himself back in.

My entire body shook as that tingling in my pussy increased. I've never met someone that could elicit this quick of a response from me before. My skin burned for him, my heat clenched at him, and my lips craved the taste of him.

Latching my mouth to his, Shane set a smooth rhythm for us, the climb to ecstasy slow and steady.

"Please don't stop," I whispered against his lips.

His gaze was intense. "I won't." He rocked into me hard, his pelvis grinding against mine, causing all sorts of wonderful sensations to course through me, from head to toe. "I can't." He withdrew almost completely, then rammed into me harder, the twisting of his hips hitting a bundle of nerves inside that had me gasping. Shane grinned down at me, his eyes displaying satisfaction. "I'm going to fuck you hard." His pace picked up. "I'm going to fuck you well." His words, his body...hell, the man in his entirety, had my body breaking out in goosebumps, my pussy glistening with its need, contracting in preparation for an orgasm I knew would most likely blind me. "And when I'm done, we're fucking doing this again until all we can do is give into the exhaustion."

With one final hard thrust, my body bowed into him as I screamed out my release.

"Holy shit! Holy fuck!" Shane groaned over me, his hips losing their rhythm. "Fucking hell!" He plunged deep and stayed rooted. "Em!" His cock jerked with warmth coating my insides, eliciting another tremor from me. My eyes stayed fused at the dazzling picture of satisfied masculinity before me. His head was tilted back, his bottom lip caught between his teeth, eyes closed. The sheen of sweat coating his chest didn't detract from his appeal. In fact, all I wanted to do was lick the man from head to toe. "My beautiful Em." His whispered words knocked me for a loop from my perusal.

My eyes darted to his. "What?"

His eyes had lost that animalistic glaze they'd possessed, and now held tenderness. "I called you my beautiful Em." He dropped a soft kiss on my lips, his hands feathering into my hair as he shifted his weight onto his elbows so as not to crush me.

*His beautiful Em?* I melted. No one had called me that before.

"Mine," he rasped, making my head jerk back.

"I—I..." I hadn't realized I'd spoken aloud.

He gave me a pointed look. "Mine," he repeated. "*My* beautiful Em." Then he took my mouth as if he owned it.

Normally, I would have run in the opposite direction at this type of possessiveness, especially after my disastrous marriage, but Shane made it feel like it was an honor, like I'd be cherished...treasured...protected. Safe.

sixteen

SHANE

MY PHONE CHIMING in my pants pocket woke me at dawn. Careful not to wake Emberlyn, I rolled over and reached for my discarded trousers to fetch it, noticing the time reading out 5:45 as I activated the screen, rolling onto my back.

MOM:

Good night?

My mother's text made me groan. *Shit!*

I looked over at a soundly sleeping Emberlyn and smiled. I hadn't planned on our night turning out the way it had, but I'd be damn crazy to say I wasn't happy at the way things ended this morning.

Set an extra plate for breakfast, please?

MOM:

Don't rush. Rosie and I stayed up late last night. You know how she is.

Oh, I knew how she was all right. She'd most likely suckered

Mom into some movie marathon of sorts, and would sleep in. I thanked my lucky stars for small reprieves, because I hadn't thought what I'd say to my daughter if she woke up to notice my absence this morning. Then again, she'd probably just chalk it up to me having had to leave for work because I was called in. It wasn't an odd occurrence.

Setting my phone on the bedside table, I rolled toward Emberlyn and wrapped my arms around her once again. The smell of us lingered on her skin. I fucking missed this. Not the sex per se, but the cuddling, sleeping in the same bed with a woman that meant something to me. Having someone to wake up with.

"Sweetheart?" I whispered against the shell of her ear.

"Mmm?" She snuggled further into me, her ass rubbing against my ever-hardening cock. To be honest, the fucking thing had been in a state of semi-arousal from the time she'd answered the door with her bum foot last night.

My arms gave her a squeeze before rolling her onto her back, hovering above her. "Christ, you're adorable when you're half asleep," I said, nuzzling her cheek, as I allowed the hand I wasn't leaning on to trace the side of her face. Her breath caught. "I want you. Sleep-warm and snuggly. Just like this."

She gave me a slow drowsy smile. "Just let me get up and brush my—"

Before she could finish, my lips crushed hers in a hard, brief kiss, then I pulled back. "You're not getting out of bed until I let you."

Her brows furrowed. "Until you let me?" Bracing her hands on my shoulders, she made to push me back. "Shane..." Her mouth snapped shut at the look I gave her.

"Sweetheart..." I grabbed first one hand, kissing its knuckles before pressing its palm to my cheek, then reached for the other, inflicting the same treatment. "It would defeat the purpose of you being in the state you currently are in if I let you out, wouldn't it?"

"I suppose you're right," she grumbled, but her arms reached around my neck, pulling me closer, not giving me the choice but to push her legs apart and maneuver my body overtop of hers.

I smirked. "Are we a grumpy pants in the morning?" I cajoled.

She groaned. "Only when I can't brush my teeth." Her nose scrunched up. "Morning breath isn't sexy."

"Em..."

Her gaze softened at my shortened version of her name. "I like that you call me that," she whispered.

"Good, because if I have my way with you in the next minute, I can guarantee you'll be hearing it a lot more before these sheets cool down." I pounced for a quick peck, before trailing my lips down her chin, saying, "Good morning," proceeding to her neck, then moving lower.

"Good morning, indeed." She sighed as I scraped my teeth along her collarbone, her legs widening to allow my hips into the cradle of her thighs.

Last night, or rather earlier this morning, after our third round, we'd fallen asleep completely naked. I was thankful for this fact as I reached down, my hand finding her heat sopping wet.

"Are you sore?" I asked her, my fingers never halting in their gentle stroking.

"Tender," she panted.

"I'll go slow," I promised, taking myself in hand and guiding my length into her core, until I was completely sheathed by her.

It was slow...lazy. I wouldn't really call it fucking either.

In the early daylight hours, I showed Emberlyn how I could be tender with her, instead of the crazed animal I had been last night.

My cock begged for release, but I wasn't giving into my urges until the woman splayed below me succumbed to hers first.

Arching down to take one of her nipples into my mouth, I tugged on it a few times before her pussy clamped down on me, and her mouth uttered my name as if it were a prayer.

That was it for me.

By the time I'd regained my faculties, I looked down to find Emberlyn's gaze trained on my face as she sported a grin, muttering, "I'm loving slow."

This had me collapsing overtop of her, laughing into the pillow next to her head.

### EMBERLYN

After Shane's stellar display of prowess last night, as well as again this morning, it was safe to say I was a little achy.

And I'd suffer some more if it wielded the same results.

*God, you're such a slut!*

The way the man had played my body, as if he was a connoisseur of fine instruments, had me able to get out of my head, stop worrying about if I was pleasing him enough, and had me firmly stuck in the moment.

During one bout of pillow talk, last night, I knew he hadn't been with anyone for nearing on a year now. Despite this, I got a sense that what we'd experienced together hadn't been anything either of us had expected. The chemistry had been explosive, and I mean the check-to-see-if-you-still-had-hair-on-your-body kind. I swear, had things gotten any hotter, I was sure we'd have burned my house down to a crisp.

"What are you thinking so hard about that's got you all flushed?" Shane's lips landed on the back of my shoulder, while his arms wrapped around me under the sprinkling water of the shower.

"Last night." My body hummed as I leaned back into his chest.

"Mmm." He scraped his teeth over the tendon at the side of

my neck, his cock standing at attention again, while it nestled in the crack of my ass. "It was a great night."

"Uh-huh." He pressed himself against me, as if I couldn't feel the steel rod twitching between our bodies. "I dare say your stamina is quite impressive."

I felt his soundless laugh through my back. "It's all you, sweetheart. I can't help the fact that you make me hard and take notice."

"Sure." I turned in his arms to face him and was met with his soft gaze.

"Come over for breakfast?" It wasn't really a question, more of a statement of sorts.

"Shane..."

"I already told Mom to set an extra place for you," he explained, "and I know Rosie would love to see you." He kissed my nose, then pulled back to gaze down at me, giving me a brief squeeze. "And I'm not ready to let you go yet."

Damn the man.

Overbearing, yes.

Controlling, sure.

Sweet...abso-fucking-lutely!

So I did what any girl in my situation—which meant, naked, wet...sated to the core, yet aching for more—would do.

"Okay," I whispered.

"Good girl." He tapped my ass playfully, all the while smirking. "Now let's get you clean so I can dirty you up again."

"You're insatiable," I said, wrapping my arms around his neck, leaning in to peck his lips.

"Keep rubbing up against me like that, sweetheart, and we'll be lucky if we make lunch." To emphasize his rather excited self, he grabbed onto both of my ass cheeks and ground his hips into mine.

And there went my libido, kicking into high gear.

# seventeen

Shane

"WHERE WERE YOU?" Rosie stomped toward the front door, hands on hips, and a mutinous look on her face as soon as Emberlyn and I walked over the threshold.

"Oh shit," I heard Emberlyn mumble under her breath at my side, but slightly behind me.

"I said," my daughter came to a stop only feet away from me, "where were you two? I've been waiting for like *forever*!"

I tried to remind my little girl of her manners. "Baby girl, won't you say hi to our guest?"

"Oh, I'll get there in a minute," she grumped. "Answer the question, Daddy."

It was near impossible to keep a straight face. She may look like her mother, but she definitely took after her father in attitude.

"Baby—"

"You're supposed to tell me when you're not coming home right away," she huffed. "I was *worried*!"

Talk about a sucker punch to the gut. My little one sure knew how to give it back.

"We've talked about this," she went on, her face a deep crimson, her eyes welling up with tears before she threw herself forward.

Bending down to catch her, imagine my surprise when she bypassed me and crashed into Emberlyn, sobbing. Mom came around the kitchen's corner, eyeing the interaction, a small smile spreading across her lips as she nodded for me to really look at the scene unfolding before us.

Plopped onto the floor, Emberlyn had my daughter on her lap, cradled against her chest, her head buried in those dark curls, that probably smelled like cotton candy, whispering to her.

"But I wanted to have the first sleepover!" she growled, turning her tearstained face toward me, making sure I didn't miss her ire. "She was my friend first, Daddy!"

My mother managed to just barely cover up the snort that accompanied her laughter, while the woman I'd just spent the most amazing night with cowered behind my little girl, her body shaking silently with her humor.

How the hell was I going to explain myself? "Lana Rose—"

"I get her next weekend," she promptly decided, Emberlyn's shocked gaze mirrored mine as they clashed together.

"Don't you think you should ask—"

"*You* didn't!" she argued.

"How's this, sweets," Emberlyn began with a soft voice, "let's see about making that happen? I'm sure your dad and Grams can use a break, so if it's okay with them, we can definitely have a sleepover next weekend. We can play games, build a fort, paint each other's toenails."

Lana Rose's nose scrunched up. "Are yours as gross as Grams', because I'm not doing that if they are."

"She has very pretty feet, baby girl," I broke into their moment, winking at Emberlyn and causing her to blush a beautiful crimson.

"On that note, I'll get the pancakes on." Humor laced my

mom's tone as she turned and disappeared back into the kitchen.

We were at the neighborhood park when the call came through, breaking me from watching Emberlyn push my Rosie on the swing set.

"Peters," I answered gruffly.

"James found something." Will hung up before I could say anything, effectively ruining the first of rare weekends I got off.

My pulse quickened, my palms grew sweaty. Could this be it? Could it be the break in the case that I needed to catch this crazed killer?

Hurrying to where both females were busy giggling, I made eye contact with Emberlyn first, her smile quickly disappeared as soon as she took in my serious expression.

"Everything okay?" she asked as soon as she made it to my side, Rosie now left to swing on her own.

"I'm sorry, but I have to go into work."

She nodded, a worried look entering her eyes. "Everything okay?" she repeated.

"We might have a break in that murder case I'm working," I said by way of explanation, just as my daughter joined us.

"Daddy, can we go for ice cream?"

"I can't, Rosie. I just got called in. I'll drop you two off at Grams', then I have to get going." I was never going to get used to the sight of my little girl's face falling in disappointment at the news that I had to leave her behind. Every time I saw that look on her face, it made me feel like shit; it never failed to serve up the appeal of Dalton's offer to buy in and work for him full-time and ditching the JPD. Something closer to a regular nine-to-five—with the minor exception, depending on the case— would make parenting a hell of a lot easier.

· · ·

I stormed into the coroner's office forty minutes after receiving Will's call.

"What do you have for us, James?" I said by way of greeting.

The man smirked. "DNA."

"You're shitting me?" I stared at the man, waiting for the camera crew to make their appearance because there was no way in hell our unsub could be that sloppy.

"It was damn well, nearly undetectable, but I wanted you two to be the first to see these results for yourselves." James handed me the report.

*Fibers found...*

*...blood DNA not matching victim's or victim's partner swabbed from laceration on left cheek...*

"Tell me you ran the sample through CODIS." I looked up at James expectantly.

The man nodded. "Page three of the report, gentlemen."

"Fuck me!" Will turned to pace. As soon as he'd reached the nearest wall, he punched it. "Goddamn motherfucker!"

*You stole the words right from my mouth, brother.*

We finally had our man.

# eighteen

EMBERLYN

*You're mine, bitch.*

THE MESSAGE SENT chills running down my spine, but it was the little bit of white lace that accompanied the embossed card, sitting atop my dresser, that drove the eerie point home.

Without a second's hesitation, I'd set the small decoupage box on the side table to the entrance and hobbled to my purse, which I'd left on the coffee table shortly after Shane had dropped me off earlier in the day. Grabbing my phone, with Stan's business card in hand, I dialed.

"Safe & SEALed, Stan speaking."

"Hi, Stan." I swallowed the growing knot in my throat, "Emberlyn Roth. I'm going ahead with the system you recommended."

"Ms. Roth, is everything okay?"

"No...no, not really. How soon do you think you can get it installed?"

"I can be there as soon as tomorrow if that works? I have everything in stock." He hesitated. "Do you need someone? I work with—"

Shit! Was I that obvious? Clearing my throat, I said, "I'll be fine. Thank you. See you tomorrow?"

"Bright and early tomorrow, how's that?" He didn't sound convinced.

"Perfect. Good night, Stan. Sorry to disturb your evening."

"Don't you worry about it, and if you—"

"I'll be okay," I assured him, or was I trying to assure myself? Nevertheless, I hung up the phone.


Thirty minutes later, there was a light knock on my front door. After hanging up with Stan, I had made my rounds, ensuring once again that my windows and doors were locked tight...and they were.

*So how did they get in?*

I even went to the point of covering every window with my curtains and blinds. I hated I was forced to do that. I was someone who liked to see the outdoors; I loved the way the dust motes danced around in the air when the sun streamed through my windows. But I felt too exposed, which meant I had to pick the lesser of all evils.

Hesitantly making my way to the front entrance, and not for the first time, I wished for a peephole to see who had come calling at a little after nine in the evening.

"Emberlyn?" I heard a soft female ask. "Ember, open up, it's Devolin and Dalton. Remember us? We met at—"

Of course I remembered them. But how had they gotten my address? As if I couldn't undo the two deadbolts on my door and release the chain fast enough, when I did, I flung my heavy wooden front door open to greet them, throwing myself straight for Dalton, who caught me.

You could say I was spooked.

"Call Shane, babe," Dalton muttered, his arms holding me upright, rubbing a soothing pattern on my back as he reversed us into my home.

"Shane?" I mumbled against him? He smelled of soap and man, much like Shane always seemed to. It was comforting, although not as comforting as…"Wait," my head snapped back so I could see the man's face, "you know Shane?"

The man set me back, lowering me to the couch as I realized he'd led us to my living room.

Crouching down in front of me, his guilty eyes met mine. "We're friends," he explained. "As for the rest, I'll let him explain things. For now, I want you to stay right here with Dev, and I'll go look around."

"Wait!" I looked between both of them. "How'd—"

"Stan called me."

# *nineteen*



CAPTAIN DODGE SLAMMED his fists down onto his desk.

"Sir?" Will attempted.

"I should have known something was up," the man chastised himself. He lifted his head, unmistakable grief and regret were strewn across his expression. "My own son," he croaked. "A murderer!"

He swiped his hands across his desk, sending papers flying everywhere. Next thing we knew, he'd fisted his stapler, flinging it across the room, where it made a sizeable hole in the drywall, and got stuck.

Nancy, the receptionist, came barging in, a look of panic on her face. "Is everything—" she began, her eyes rounding when she witnessed the damage to the wall.

"I'm sorry, Nance," Dodge said. "Everything's fine here."

The woman eyed me, then Will; next was James. She didn't seem convinced but beat a retreat regardless.

"Cap—" I started.

"You're sure?" he whispered, eyeing James specifically.

"I ran the results three times, sir," he explained. "There's no doubt in my mind that your son was at the scene. Since he wasn't on shift when the investigation took place, I can't say that he's guilty, but I can say there's cause for suspicion."

"Bring him in," the older man ordered.

Nodding to the captain, James was first to leave the office, followed by Will, then myself. "Peters..."

I turned at the door to find my troubled boss's eyes filling with tears. "Yeah?"

"I wish I—"

"Boss, this isn't on you." My voice cracked, knowing all too well what he was hinting at.

"But—"

"No!" I argued. "If this is going down the way I think it will, you're staying clear of this. This isn't on you, Cap, it's all on him."

The man gave me a feeble nod.

Once I was assured that no other word would follow, I turned my back on my boss and walked out, grumbling, "Let's go get the son of a bitch," to Will as I passed by him.

Hindsight was twenty-twenty, as it always seemed to be. I should have known to warn dispatch to keep the APB on Casen on the down low, on the off chance the fucktard was listening in on the radio.

By the time we got to Casen Dodge's apartment, the bastard was nowhere to be found. A neighbor reported hearing all sorts of crashing noises coming from his place about ten minutes prior to our arrival, however. She'd seen him storm out of his apartment and head out like his pants were lit on fire.

Running my hands through my hair and pulling at the strands, my frustration came out in a loud roar as I kicked the cruiser's tire.

"I want to use him for target practice," I growled, "then rip him limb from limb, starting by shoving his dick down his throat, making him choke on it."

"I'm sure the entire force will be wanting to get their licks in with the fucker before this is over," Will attested.

"Let's get out of here." I opened the driver's side door and got in. When Will was settled into his seat, I looked over at him. "Call the judge and get a warrant for his apartment. I want a trace on his phones. I want to know if he's got anyone in his corner who can possibly cover for him. We already know that Cap can't provide the manpower on this one, so I'm siccing Dalton on the case, red tape be damned."

It wasn't until we'd gotten back to the precinct that I could no longer ignore the vibrating coming from my phone. Still sitting in the driver's seat, I pulled it out of my pocket, shocked to find I had ten missed calls and five messages. All of them from Dalton.

*What the fuck?*

I hit the button that connected me to my voicemail.

*"Shane, it's Devolin, Stan called Dalton. Something's up with Emberlyn. Kip and I are heading over to check things out. Call us."*

My heart started palpitating.

*"Peters, you need to check your messages. Call pronto."*

*"Shane, it's Devolin again. I think you really need to come to Emberlyn's place when you get this."*

*"Your woman needs you. Get your ass in gear, brother."*

"Shit."

"Everything okay?" Will asked.

"No," I mumbled, as I listened to the last message.

*"Shane, man..."* Dalton growled. *"I'm about to lose my shit with your woman's ex. Where the fuck are you?"*

"What the fuck?" I punched to disconnect, threw my phone onto my dash, then rubbed my hands down my face on a sigh.

"What's up?"

I shook my head. There were too many things happening at once. "I need to go," I croaked, feeling every bit of my body slowing down with exhaustion but more so with frustration. "Talk to Cap. Find out if Casen's got any other properties he may have access to. When that's done, call Judge Mason and get the damn search warrants. Get whoever you need at the precinct on this to pitch in if you have to. I don't care how you do it, just do it by the book. I'll talk to Dalton when I find a minute. I'm needed at home."

Dropping my partner off at the precinct, I left him and our ongoing investigation in my rearview mirror with a panicked sensation coursing through me, filling me with dread for what I was going to happen onto next.

# twenty

**EMBERLYN**

"EVERYTHING CHECKS OUT on your property. I've made sure that your windows and doors were locked in your cottage," Dalton said, announcing his arrival from making his rounds.

"Thank you." I bowed my head, feeling helpless and discouraged that someone had to come to my aid instead of being able to help myself.

"Tell him, Ember," Devolin urged me.

"Tell me what?" Dalton's features darkened, as if he knew that what I'd have to say next wouldn't be good.

"Something was delivered today, while Shane, Rosie, and I were out," I whispered.

"What?" he asked.

I nodded toward the front door. "It's on the table over there."

Devolin was the first to leave my side and came back handling the small box, the scrap of lace hanging out from one side, with the lid tilted sideways. The disturbed look on her face said enough. "Some creep is sending you underwear?" she squeaked out.

Dalton pinched the bridge of his nose, taking a deep breath and releasing it with a long drawn out, "Fuck."

"It's from my ex," I explained.

"This isn't the first time, is it?" I shook my head to indicate the negative as an answer to the man's question. "Where are the others?"

"Garage," I rasped, my throat having gone dry. "Top shelf on the left wall. White storage bin."

Dalton disappeared.


To have Dalton riffling through that bin of things which had been delivered over the last few weeks was humiliating.

He wasn't a friend.

He wasn't really an acquaintance either.

I may have felt safe with him and Devolin here with me, but as he pulled one item out after the other, albeit in a clinical and assessing way, what with his wearing latex gloves, it only solidified the fact that by the time Shane got here, I'd be in a shitload of trouble.

The pounding on my front door had me jumping out of my skin, while Devolin soothingly rubbed at my upper back to calm me down.

Dalton sat what was one of the many letters I'd received on the table before righting himself. "I'll get that."

Beyond a door opening and shutting, I didn't hear anything else for the next few minutes.


When Shane made his approach, our eyes connecting, I couldn't hold it together anymore. I broke down, a sobbing mess collapsing into his chest just as soon as he'd kneeled in front of me.

"Shhh." He tightened his hold on me. "I'm sorry I wasn't here sooner, but I'm here now, Em. We'll figure this all out. I promise."

"You know?" I hiccupped, pulling away enough to tilt my head up to look him in the eyes.

"Dalton filled me in a little," he growled.

"I don't know how he got in," I whispered. "I'm scared, Shane. I did everything right. I changed my numbers, I moved... I don't even use the same email address."

He cupped my face, wiping at my tears with his thumbs as he stared at me intently. "We'll get Brycen on the phone."

"Already done," Dalton said. "I couldn't wait for you, so I put him on task."

Shane nodded. "Send me the bill."

"Family doesn't pay," he grunted. Shane and I turned to face the man, who met my gaze head on. "This one is personal."

"But—" I protested.

Dalton's gaze was unwavering and brokered no argument.

"Em, let him," Shane whispered over my temple before kissing it.

I sighed in exasperation. "Oh, all right!" I turned to look at Devolin. "Are they always so...so—"

"Bossy?" the woman supplied with a grin.

"Yes!"

"Most of the time," she answered breezily. "But they're right on the money this time, hon. That jackass ex of yours will cease to exist once NSI is done with him."

Dalton's phone bleeped an incoming call warning. Hitting a button, he said, "You've got D, Dev, Peters, and Ember. This better be good news."

"Out?" I felt as though an elephant had taken residence on my chest. I struggled to catch my breath with no avail. Having him know where I lived was one thing, but him being out changed things; made them more real.

Trevor Sykes was granted early parole due to overcrowding, it seemed. I knew the judicial system was less than perfect, but I never expected to have it fail me.

"Why wasn't she contacted?" Shane barked at the phone sitting between all of us on my coffee table.

"Seems like Emberlyn's lawyer is currently on medical leave. Something has to be said about an active job and lifestyle. I guess sitting behind a desk, gobbling up rich foods, and drinking too much, is bound to catch you in the ticker at some point," Brycen said. "The guy had a heart attack, leading him to a triple bypass. He's currently at home and was none the wiser as to what's happened with Ember's case until I spoke with him."

"How long?" I gulped, then cleared my throat. "How long has he been out?"

"Ten days," Brycen confirmed over the line.

Ten days.

That explains the sudden escalation in deliveries. What it didn't explain though, was why all of a sudden the letters? Most of his gifts always had short notes and those were still present. The solitary letters were new, however.

"What is it, sweetheart?" Shane urged me. "I can tell you're holding something back."

"The letters." I shook my head. "They don't sound like him."

Shane turned to Dalton, leaving Devolin at my side.

Dalton spread out each and every letter in their respective baggies.

It took him about ten minutes of reading and rereading them before he came back to my side. "I can't say whether it's the same person or not. Both notes and letters are typed up, but I trust what you're saying." I nodded in appreciation of his faith in my analysis. "Can you give us a timeframe as to when the gifts started, in comparison to when the letters did?"

"The gifts stopped after I sold, then moved out of our marital home. They started up about a month ago." I gave a quick, cursory glance to all three of my companions. "The letters started over the last week."

"Since there's no postmark, Bryce, I'm going to send this in so we can see about getting some prints," Dalton told us. "Matthews, I expect you to get in touch with either me or Shane whenever you dig something up on Sykes. I want to know where he's at, who his parole officer is, if he's got a job..."

"On it, boss. Out." The discernible click of Brycen hanging up was followed by Dalton disconnecting the call on our end.

"Right..." Dalton's eyes were trained on me. "I think we can agree that you're not safe in this house by yourself. Until Stan can get your security system up and running, I want you to stay with someone."

"She'll stay with me." Shane's statement came out as if it was law.

"What?" I stared at him. "No! I—I can't put you out like that."

"Em," Shane began softly, "sweetheart, what makes you think you'd be putting me out?"

"What will your mother think? And what about Rosie?" I asked. "I'm not safe, and Trevor clearly knows where I'm at. I don't want to bring this trouble to you and your family." I shook my head, then looked at Dalton. "Is there another option? Can't I stay in a hotel for the next few nights? Something kind of like a witness protection thing? I have a gun...And what about my business? I have clients...obligations I need to meet."

"She can stay with us," Devolin blurted, while rubbing her large belly, "can't she, Kip?"

"I'm not bringing this shitstorm your way, either," I argued. "I appreciate everything you're all doing for me, I do, but I can't have you guys in the crossfire either."

"You're not going to a fucking hotel, Em, not unless I'm with you," Shane argued. "We can pack your bags, then head over to mine so I can pack some necessities, then we'll go to a hotel if you're that worried about Mom and Rosie. And about work, if you'd agree to stay at mine, then you'd still be able to work out of Mom's kitchen until Stan's done his work. There's no way I want you here alone. We'll talk about you having a gun later." He grabbed my chin gently, making sure to look me in the eyes. "So what's it gonna be, sweetheart?"

# *twenty-one*

**S**HANE

THE SILENCE of the night was broken, waking me from sleep. Laying in the dark, I allowed myself to concentrate on what it was I had heard.

Footsteps.

The creaking of a door.

More footsteps, fading as they moved away from my bedroom.

A light switch.

A cabinet door shutting.

Running water.

The scraping of a chair.

Rolling over toward my alarm clock, I saw that it was just after two o'clock in the morning. Only one person could be awake at this time of night: our new houseguest.

Pushing back my covers, I quickly slipped into a pair of jogging shorts and headed toward the kitchen, finding Emberlyn seated at the table, staring into a full glass of water.

The floor creaked beneath my feet as I moved toward her,

gaining her attention. Emberlyn's eyes were sunken and red-rimmed. Seeing her like this broke my heart.

"Can't sleep?" I asked the obvious.

She shook her head. "I can't seem to settle." I turned her chair so I could crouch down between her legs, my hands smoothing over her bare thighs. "My mind won't stop whirling with everything that's going on."

"Anything I can do?"

Her eyes softened as her hand reached out and cupped my face. "You're doing it right now. Just being here, Shane, it's more than I deserve."

"Sweetheart..." My words hung as I regained my feet and pulled her up to hers so we stood chest-to-chest. I wrapped my arms around her the moment she cuddled into me. "Come to bed."

Her head snapped back so she could look up at me. "I can't do that. Your mom and Rosie are here."

"I don't care." I pecked her forehead. "You need your sleep, and I don't think you'll find it unless you feel safe." She didn't answer, which told me I was right. "If it'll make you feel better, I'll set my alarm to make sure we're awake before everyone else. They'll never know you didn't spend the night in the spare room."

After pondering my words for a short moment, she brushed her lips tenderly against mine and whispered, "Okay." As she led me toward the stairs, allowing me to turn the lights off as we went, she paused and turned toward me. "Tomorrow, we'll have to have a chat about your bossiness. I'm still not happy about your strong-arming me to stay here, you know."

I let out a low chuckle. "Sure thing, sweetheart. Sure thing. And while we're at it, we'll cover how you've been packin'."

"Shane!" she whisper-scolded.

"Get that fine ass of yours to bed, woman, or I'll carry you there myself."

On a huffed, "Boneheaded caveman," she preceded me up the stairs.

You know you're exhausted when your alarm goes off, you heard it, but turned the damn thing off, rolled over, and drifted off again.

That's exactly what happened later that morning; at least until I heard the door to my bedroom creak open, revealing my daughter. Her eyes widened when she spotted Emberlyn lying curled up with her back to my chest.

I lifted my index finger to my lips, in indication for her to be quiet, and motioned for her to come closer.

"Daddy, what's Ember doing here?" she whispered.

"I asked her to come and stay with us because her house is getting some work done, and it's not safe for her to be there right now," I explained. She didn't need to know the details. Being the daughter of a detective—the kid of any cop really—I noticed our respective offspring seemed to age beyond their years far too quickly. I was already seeing this effect on my girl, and if I could shield her from unnecessary troubles, I damn well would.

"Why are you holding her? You only do that when I have bad dreams." Her eyes rounded at her nine-year-old realization. "Did she have a bad dream?"

*Thank you, Rosie.* Her statement provided me with an out on my fuck up. One I doubted Emberlyn would be impressed with, seeing as I'd failed to wake her up for her bed switch like I'd promised her last night.

"She did," I said softly.

"Can I help chase her bad dream away?" She bit her lip, evidently thinking I'd refuse her the sweet gesture. "Please?"

This had me smiling. I fucking loved my little girl and her thoughtfulness. "I think she'd like that, princess." I pulled her head toward me so I could press my lips against her forehead. "Very much. Now, climb on up here."

Careful not to jostle the mattress, Rosie crawled toward Emberlyn's still body and curled herself to her front, tucking the top of her head just below her chin. My smile turned to a full-out grin as soon as one of Emberlyn's arm wrapped itself around and pulled my daughter in tight against her on a contented sigh.

After a few moments of watching the two, I settled back down, letting sleep take me away once more.

# twenty-two



THE SWEET SMELL of strawberry mixed with cotton candy was the first indication that I wasn't where I should have been.

The tiny furnace-like body I was currently cuddling to my front was my second.

And the third—a *big* third—was the fact I had a large boiler tucked against my back, his muscular arms wrapped around me, tightening ever so slightly the more I came to.

Shane's lips met the back of my neck, pressing lightly. "Good morning," he rasped.

My heart was beating out of my chest with the reality of where I was and who I was with.

Lifting my head slowly, I peered down. I'd be lying if I said I wasn't on the verge of freaking out.

Shane's arms gave me a brief squeeze. "Relax," he whispered. "She came in and saw you. I explained that you were having work done to your place and it wasn't safe to stay there."

"I shouldn't be in here!" I whisper-yelled. "You said you'd wake me."

"Shhh."

"Don't *shhh* me!"

His body shook against mine in silent laughter. "She thought I was cuddling you because of a nightmare. She asked if she could help me chase your bad dream away, like I do with hers."

My body lost its sudden rigidity as I melted back into the bed, into the two Peters I was sandwiched between. My heart warmed. I found myself leaning down and pressing a soft kiss to Lana Rose's crown.

"I hope you're not mad." Shane's words tickled the back of my neck.

"I was." What was the point in lying? "But I'm not now."

"Ember?" Little Rosie mumbled as she began to stir.

"Right here, sweets," I said softly.

"Did the bad dream go away?" She had yet to open her eyes, instead she simply cuddled in closer to me.

"It did." I pressed another kiss to the top of her head. "Thank you."

"Good." I couldn't see her mouth, with her tight position against me, but I could hear the smile in her singular word. "Daddy said you'll be staying with us for a few days. Can we have a sleepover in Daddy's room again tonight?"

Shane snorted, his body shaking once more with laughter.

This had me smiling.

Was this what a real family felt like? The reality of the moment had an imaginary deadweight lifting off of the pit of my gut. I'd been robbed of this dream. Suddenly, the fleeting thought of losing what was right there surrounding me this morning, my arms tightened around the little girl as I snuggled her, much like my mother used to. This set off a chain reaction because no sooner than my grip grew, so did Shane's on me.

. . .

Nora had left a little over an hour before to join a few friends for coffee, as well as run errands for the family. Shane had gone into work after briefly allowing me to escort him to my little cottage to bring back some supplies, as well as packaging materials, so I could finalize a few orders at some point during the day.

So far, Rosie and I have managed to perform facials on each other and paint our toenails. I had to admit, my feet looked as if a bubble gum machine puked all over them after the girl was done with them, but I would wear that messy job with pride. It was things like that, which one would never think they'd missed out on until they were faced with it. My sudden bout of melancholy at never having this with a daughter of my own faded quickly because Lana Rose had given that to me.

We were in the middle of watching the first of the *Harry Potter* movies when I realized we needed extra ribbon.

"Sweets, I need to run back over to the cottage for a few minutes," I told her.

"But you promised Daddy you wouldn't go there by yourself." She bit her lip.

I escorted her to the front door, pointing out the window to Stan's van sitting in my driveway. As promised, the man had shown up bright and early to get started on my deluxe security system.

"You see? Stan is there. I'll be quick." I cupped her cheek. "Promise."

She nodded hesitantly. "Okay, but be super fast, Ember. I don't want us to get in trouble."

I couldn't help the smile. It was cute that she was trying to protect me from her father's wrath. I'd deal with Shane when, or if, the time came.

Sliding on my flip-flops, I kissed Lana Rose's forehead and made my way out the door. I could feel the girl's eyes on my back. Once I crossed the street, I peered toward the Peters' house before turning the corner for the backyard, seeing her still watching from the window at the side of the front door.

I had just locked the cottage's door when I was shoved forcefully against it, my face slamming nose first into its frame.

*What the fuck?*

The force of the blow had me seeing stars and my world began to spin like a tilt-a-whirl.

"Stay away from the cop, if you know what's good for you," a husky voice I didn't recognize spat into my ear. The stench of stale liquor on his breath had me forcing back bile. "You're not her. You'll never be her. The bastard deserves all the misery he gets. No one fucks with me."

As quick as he appeared, he was gone, leaving me to collapse onto the ground—frozen in fear—ribbons and tags scattered all around me. I tried to calm myself and assess the situation at hand, but it was no use, my lungs wouldn't have it. Black spots crowded my vision, and darkness blanketed me as my breath grew shorter and shorter, until all I saw was darkness.

A child sobbing nearby was the first thing I heard when I came to.

"It's okay, Rosie." Stan's voice was soft. "She's waking up, see?" A sniffle. "Emberlyn, can you hear me?"

My head pounded the moment I cracked my eyes open. With the fact that I was the one in charge of Lana Rose, and the poor thing was in a panic, I pushed through the pain, lifting my hand up to my forehead to shield my eyes from some of the sudden brightness.

"I'm okay," I mumbled, then tried to sit up with Stan's help. "Just a bump, sweets." I reached for my nose, wincing at the immediate tenderness that made my eyes water, and groaned, "Ouch."

"The ambulance is on the way," Stan informed me. "And so is Shane."

*Shit.*

Well now I've gone and done it.

# twenty-three

SHANE

I SWEAR that damn woman was out to give me a heart attack.

When I'd picked up the fucking phone, displaying Stan's number, I knew that trouble had found at least one of my girls before I'd answered the thing. I could feel it in my gut.

*Fucking woman!*

Panic to ensure that both Emberlyn and Rosie were safe had me rushing out of the precinct with Will on my tail, barely making it to the cruiser on time, heading toward home.

"Relax, man," Will said as we were a few blocks away from our destination. "You heard the radio. Ambulance is on the way, and it doesn't seem like it's anything major, other than a broken nose."

The picture my mind painted of Ember with black and blue eyes, a swollen nose, blood dripping and smeared all over the front of her, and whatever else my head could conjure up on top of that, was enough to make my foot press harder on the gas.

"Don't you fucking tell me to relax, Will. If it were Tina, would you relax?"

At the mention of his wife, he groaned. "Good point."

"Yeah. Didn't think so," I mumbled as I pulled up to the curb in front of Emberlyn's house, the ambulance already in the drive, its back doors open. Sitting on the ambulance's rear bumper, I could see my woman holding a large piece of gauze over her nose, while Stan had Rosie on his lap, both watching over my woman who spoke to both of them.

Jumping out of the car, I heard Rosie break out in a loud giggle at something Emberlyn told her. At the same time, Will slapped my shoulder and stopped beside me, assessing the scene.

"Just saying, but if you don't keep her, you've got a few more screws loose than I ever thought. That baby girl of yours likes everyone, but even Tina can't make that kid laugh like that." He didn't wait for my response and kept walking toward the trio and the emergency vehicle.

### EMBERLYN

"Where are you going?" Lana Rose's little voice broke me away from the bag I was packing.

"I have to go, sweets." After today, I'd proven to be a useless friend, not to mention a crap potential girlfriend, and an even worse neighbor. Nothing that happened today should have occurred. And none of it would have had I'd done *what I was told* —according to Shane—and stayed put, as he told me on our way back from the emergency room after having my nose snapped back in place.

He was right.

I was wrong.

I was always wrong.

I have no idea why I even entertained the thought it would ever change. My ex made a point to repetitively remind me, for so many years.

So here I was, packing my bags with a heavy heart while Shane had gone somewhere—who knows where—to cool off from our argument, and his mother was supposed to be occupying Rosie, who had crept up unannounced.

I couldn't turn to face the little girl, who meant the world to me, but I had to say something. "I'm going back home."

"But, why?" Oh shit! Not tears! I didn't deal well with tears, especially when I was the cause for them to begin with.

*Why do you have to be such an idiot?*

I had to make things right.

Taking a deep breath to strengthen myself, I turned and found a teary-eyed girl staring back at me, biting her lip as if to keep her tears at bay.

"Sweets, I can't stay here." On a sigh, I made my approach and crouched down to be at the same level as her face. "I don't want to go into too many details, but me being here isn't safe for you or your grams. I should have fought your dad a bit harder about that, and for what happened today, I'm so sorry." I cupped her cheeks in both my hands.

"I want you to stay," she whined. "Daddy says that we're stronger as a team than when we're on our own."

Smart girl.

"And he's right, sweets." I bit my lip to figure out what to say next, but she beat me to the punch.

"Is it because you don't want to be our friend anymore?"

Damn but this girl was undoing me. What did I say to that?

"Oh, sweets," I pulled her in for a hug and crushed her against my chest, kissing the top of her head, then buried my face in that subtle strawberry-scented hair of hers. "You'll always have a friend in me. I hope you know that. And whenever you need me, I'll be—"

"You'll be where exactly?"

*Shit.*

I seemed frozen in place, and I couldn't seem to bring

myself to let go of Rosie to look the imposing man standing before us in the eyes.

"I asked you a question, Em," Shane ground out. "Where were you planning to go just now?"

"I—I..." I climbed to my feet, releasing Lana Rose and backing away from the two Peters crowding the only exit to the guestroom.

Shane made to follow my withdrawal, his eyes dark and intense. "You what?" he pushed.

"It's safer," I whispered.

"Rosie, go help Grams out in the kitchen," Shane said gently, but never once tore his gaze away from mine. "Em and I need to have a little talk."

"Don't be mean, Daddy," she ordered him, "but set her straight."

"A talk?" I sputtered.

Shane's eyes were still locked on me as he slowly kept coming closer. "Yes, a talk."

"Promise, Daddy." Rosie made her presence still known.

"Promise," Shane said with finality.

"Set her straight," the little girl repeated.

"I will, princess."

This made me look past the man of the house—toward his little girl—who now sported a conspiratorial gleam to her eyes. She met my gaze head on and jutted out her chin in a stubborn fashion, right before she made her exit, closing the bedroom door behind her on a low snicker. She may be all of her mother in looks, but that expression right there, that had been all Shane Peters to a T.

**SHANE**

I knew I'd been overly hotheaded with Emberlyn the moment I saw her eyes lose the glimmer they always seemed to carry. Her expression had become withdrawn, and all emotion seemed to have disappeared altogether. She'd shut down entirely.

The moment she walked toward the guestroom—her room —I knew I had fucked up royally. It's why I'd left the house as soon as she'd left the room.

I needed to calm down.

Reassess.

Think.

Then make things right again.

But when I'd made my return half an hour after I'd left the house, I hadn't expected Emberlyn to be packing her bags. Nor had I anticipated the deep-seated feeling of loss that threatened me to a breaking point.

"You're not leaving," I said a little too tersely, as soon as I heard the snick of the bedroom door announce its closed status.

"Well, I can't stay." She crossed her arms over her chest. The hurt in her eyes couldn't be missed. I'd done that to her.

*Fix it!*

I sighed, letting my head drop to my chest, and I shook it out of sheer frustration. I knew that if I let her leave, things would never be the same again.

I'd lose her.

I just knew it.

And I found myself seeing all the more clearly right in that moment.

I had a fight on my hands.

# twenty-four



I WASN'T QUITE sure what to expect, but the look of absolute devastation in Shane's expression; the sadness in his eyes, after Lana Rose left us alone, took my breath away.

To be honest, I didn't want to leave; but I couldn't stay and be part of something he didn't want me to be a part of. He'd said as much before he left the house. What's more, I couldn't be the cause of mistrust and worry—or worse—the one to blame should his mother, Rosie, or even he was to ever get hurt, with all the bullshit raining down on me as of late.

There's no way he'd ever forgive me.

Hell, there's no way I'd ever forgive myself.

If things cleared up, then maybe I'd entertain spending more time with the Peters' clan, but for now, distance was the only thing I could think of to keep them all out of harm's way.

Gulping the lump lodged in my throat, I knew I was about to crush my own hopes of something greater in my life, and it was going to hurt. No matter my intention, a man, his little girl, and his mother would end up suffering too.

It was better to end things then before they got even more complicated.

*Aren't they complicated already?*

"We've already been through this," I started. "I told you I didn't want to put your mother and daughter in danger. The same goes for you, Shane. It's why I didn't want to come here. It's why I'm not going to Dalton and Devolin's either."

He groaned. "You're sure as shit not going home."

"I can stay in a hotel for the next day, until Stan is done installing everything. Rosie helped me out with packaging. All I have left to do are the deliveries," I announced.

"Like fuck!" He took three large strides to bring us toe-to-toe.

"Shane!" came out sounding a little breathless.

His hands gripped my elbows, pulling me so our fronts touched, the scent of him swirling around my head, making me dizzy with want to simply curl up into him and let him handle everything; the way I knew he wanted.

Soft hands rubbed up my arms. "Em," he whispered. "*My Em*," came out as a growl along with a fire lighting up his eyes.

*Uh! Oh!*

"Sha—"

His lips came crashing down to mine. His tongue fought for entry, which I granted all too eagerly.

Mint and coffee.

Man and woods.

Soft to hard.

Would there ever be a time I wouldn't want him? All it took was once and where our physical chemistry was concerned, I was a goner.

"You can't leave," he panted against my jugular, my head tilting back as his lips caressed the tender skin of my neck.

"I can," I breathed.

"Don't leave me, Em."

That, right there, was why I had to. If I gave in then, I'd

never leave. If I did as he wished, I'd fall for him, his beautiful little girl, and his feisty mother, who I already adored far too much. Hell, I was already convinced I loved Rosie as though she were my own.

Distracted by my thoughts, Shane brought me back to the present as soon as his hands reached for the hem of my shirt and began to inch it up.

"I—I have to go." My body was overheating.

"Stay." Shane's eyes bored into mine. "You belong here. With me. With Rosie." He punctuated each sentence with a kiss down my sternum, until he had no other choice but to lower himself down to his knees. Large hands held my hips as he nuzzled my tummy. His tenderness brought tears to my eyes.

*Just once more.*

Cupping the side of his face so he'd look up at me, I capitulated. "Okay." I'd give him this one last time. Then I'd make sure he and his would be safe.

### SHANE

I'm not sure what it was about this time, but despite the small victory in getting Emberlyn to stay, something felt out of place. Oddly enough, it felt like the beginning of the end somehow. This only supplied me with enough determination to hopefully change things, once and for all. The woman had given into me a little too easily just now. Something told me she was still on the fence and debating to pull a runner.

*Focus!*

Emberlyn worked her magic as she stepped back from me and peeled her jeans off her legs. How the woman made hopping on one foot to get that tight shit off look sexy, I had no idea, but she had me salivating while she did it.

Once her denim was on the floor, I pounced.

She fell back to bounce onto the bed, her legs dangling off

the end of it, while I made my way between her thighs, my nose pressed to the damp spot of her white lace underwear.

"Fuck, I love your smell," I growled before licking her over the thin material. She arched into me. Using a hand, I pressed her torso into the mattress and spread my palm over her lower belly. "Stay. I want you like this." I licked my lips while massaging her pussy with my other hand. "Soft. Warm. Ripe and juicy," I growled the last.

"God, Shane," she whispered. "I swear you could have me coming apart if you kept talking like this."

Her words had me smirking. "We'll have to try that sometime." I gingerly removed my hand, making sure she stayed in place, as I grabbed the sides to her underwear and pulled tight until the lace ripped apart.

"Shane!" Her eyes were wide with shock, but heat swirled in them.

Grinning, I held the destroyed underwear in my hand and took one last sniff before tossing them over my shoulder with a nonchalant, "What?"

"Fuck," she collapsed back to the mattress, "that was too fucking hot to even get mad at you for: destroying a new pair of underwear."

"We can solve that problem quite easily." I petted her silken, wet folds.

"Mmm?"

"Just don't wear any." Before she could humor me with a response, I dove right in, causing her to squeal her surprise. "Shhh...we're not alone," I reminded her.

"Oh fuck!" She tried to scramble up the mattress, but I wasn't letting up, or letting her go, pulling her back to where she originally was.

"Stay."

Throwing an arm up, Emberlyn reached for whatever she could find. Her hand landed on a throw pillow, which she hurriedly shoved into her face.

A minute later, I was grinning like the cat that ate the cream, my chin glistening with the juices of her orgasm, barely muffled by the frilly pillow she had in a death grip.

Hurrying to peel off every stitch of clothes I had on, I slowly climbed atop Emberlyn as she made room for me in the cradle of her thighs, surrounding me with her arms.

She shocked me as she pulled my head down and gave my chin a long leisurely lick, then settled to nibble my lower lip before pulling back.

"Mmm," she smirked. "I like the way I taste on you."

"You do, do you?"

"Mm-hmm, but I love what you do to me more."

"That works out quite well, my beautiful Em," I told her, slicking my cock in her wet folds. Her eyes were ablaze with lust, but tenderness shone through. "I love what I do to you too." I kissed her hard, then pulled back and fused my eyes to hers again. "And I'm hoping you'll love what we're about to do together a whole lot more."

"Always," she whispered, her eyes now glistening as I grabbed my straining cock and slowly guided myself into her, all the while looking into her eyes.

"So perfect," I nuzzled her cheek with mine when I bottomed out. "Perfect for me." I withdrew and slid back in. "In every way."

"Shane..."

My lips captured hers as I set a slow rhythm for us. My crazed desperation was still there, but having feasted on her like a beast in heat, I found myself more eager to take things slow; to savor her.

And savor her I did.

# *twenty-five*

EMBERLYN

HE GAVE ME THE ANIMAL.

He gave me the romantic.

Fuck, but he gave it all to me; and what did I do? I left the warm cocoon of his bed, shoved on my clothes, grabbed my partially packed bag, and hightailed it out of there like the hounds of hell were all over my ass.

In retrospect, I know I shouldn't have left like I did.

*You could have left a note.*

I could have, but that would have taken too much time. Waiting for him to leave for work would have made things that much more unbearable. As it was, it had been hard enough to leave his warmth, to say nothing of making my exit from his house without his daughter and mother noticing.

But someone had noticed, despite my efforts.

Those laugh lines crinkled with disapproval the moment my eyes locked with hers from the safety of my driver's seat. Shane's mother had made me.

. . .

Now, I was sitting in some crappy hotel—I had to pinch pennies for that new high-tech security system that was being installed after all—analyzing the day's turn of events.

I knew Shane had spoken out of the heat of the moment. There's no way a man like him would make love to me the way that he had—and it had been lovemaking—after having pleaded that I stay, if he didn't trust me around his family. There's no way he'd still want me around, if I were really stupid, in his opinion. Or maybe I was after all and had proven it because I'd left him, sneaking away like a thief in the night.

Regret was potent in that moment; yet it wasn't enough to make me pick up my incessant ringing phone.

Not for him.

Not for Dalton...or Devolin.

Hell, he'd even sicced Stan on me.

I'd even turned off the locator option on the damn thing so no one could trace me. A little something I'd learned from Devolin in passing.

*Smart girl, that one.*

Yeah, I had to be stupid...


It's funny how an entire sleepless night spent atop a lumpy mattress, questionably stinky sheets, and bad TV will do to one's way of thinking.

Clarity hit at about four o'clock in the morning. I couldn't take the regret anymore, so I sat up and began to plan.

I still hadn't spoken to the police yet, Shane having promised to bring me in to give my statement this morning. The perks of being taken in by a cop, I suppose. Needless to say, he and I hadn't spoken about what exactly had happened either, or what the man had said to me, seeing as we were too busy fighting—then making up. And then I'd left him high and dry. My running off definitely was rash.

There was a lot to talk about, and my intuition told me that yesterday's attack had something to do with Shane's ongoing murder investigation. My gut churned as the memory of those photographs strewn across my neighbor's floor played over in my mind.

*Maybe I can help him out by way of apology?*

By the time I'd gathered up the courage to go back, it was midmorning. Of course, the small package with *his* usual creepy note which was delivered at my room's door—nothing but a knock, and no soul to be seen—had solidified my intent on going back to where I'd be safer.

Hell, with leaving in the way that I had, I hadn't even grabbed my gun.

So that's what I did.

Getting home had been easy enough.

Dragging my feet toward Shane's house, however, became harder as Nora came to a stop on her doorstep; arms crossed over her ample chest, gracing me with a hard look, her lips in a thin line.

After a rather uncomfortable stare down, Nora moved to the side to allow me entry. "He's waiting for you in the kitchen."

"Nora—"

She stopped my forward progress with a light hand on my arm as soon as I'd crossed the threshold. "He was devastated this morning when he found you gone, honey. I'm not one to meddle, but he's my son and he's been through enough. If you're not serious about you two, it's best you let him go. He doesn't quite know it yet, but I know it by the way he looks at you, Ember. He's in love with you."

My eyes widened. "What?"

"I know my son. He's not willing to admit it, because Lord

knows the man is stubborn, but if he isn't in love with you yet, he's sure as hell on his way." Letting go of my arm, she urged me further into her home as she closed the door behind us. "Kitchen, honey. Best get this done and over with before anything else comes up."

# *twenty-six*

Shane

I WAS busy mulling things over in my morning coffee, which had gone tepid from lack of consumption, when I peered up and saw the object of my current frustration.

Dishevelled, dark circles under her eyes, worry lines framing that luscious mouth of hers, Emberlyn never looked more beautiful than right then.

Three hours spent worrying and blaming myself for causing her to run, despite my intent being the opposite.

One hundred and eighty minutes spent thinking that I'd never see her again.

Ten-thousand-eight-hundred seconds of not knowing where she had disappeared off to; never responding to any of my calls, messages, or anyone else I'd set on her.

All those facts had me feeling antsy to the point I made to get to my feet.

Emberlyn lifted a hand. "Don't." She swallowed hard. "Just let me get this out."

Settling into my chair, I gave her a curt chin lift, hoping my face, my eyes wouldn't betray the portrayal of hardness I hoped she was seeing.

"First, I'd like to say I'm sorry," she began. "I was stupid to run off like I did. I was stupid to have gone to the cottage to get more supplies when I'd already promised I would wait." She hiccupped, her eyes shining with unshed tears. "What I'm most sorry about is the fact that I not only knowingly put myself in danger, but I left your daughter open to that same danger." The bag slung over her shoulder, along with her purse, dropped hard to the floor before she fisted her hair and let out a frustrating cry. "Goddammit, Shane! What if she'd been right there with me? What if I'd brought her along?" She began to pace, her breathing having grown heavy. "I'm so fucking stupid! Stupid! Stupid! Stupid!"

I croaked out, "Em."

"No!" She turned her tearstained face my way, her skin blotchy and red. "Is this the kind of person you want around your family? God! I don't know the first thing about being a responsible caregiver. Fuck, I'm still learning how to be in control of my own fucking life!"

"Emberlyn." I got up but didn't make a move toward the woman, who was all too busy with her tirade.

"I'm useless. It's why I wanted to leave. It's why I left, Shane," she whispered, her bottom lip quivering, indicating that her tears were far from done. "But you see? There are some things that I'm good at, and that's why I came back. Once I'm done helping you out, then I'll be out of your hair." She bit her bottom lip. "I promised Rosie I'd always be her friend." Her eyes met mine with fierceness. "I'm not breaking that promise, Shane. I swear. But where you and I are concerned—"

That's when I lunged around the kitchen table and grasped her elbows tightly. "Don't you stand there and tell me what will or won't happen, Emberlyn Roth," I growled. "Don't you dare promise my daughter something that means *everything* to her, yet deny me—*us*—the same courtesy. How can you be so sure of one and not the other, when Rosie and I are a package deal?" Her eyes rounded at my words. "That's right, Em. It's not just Rosie or just me. It's the both of us. So if you can stand there and say that you'll maintain your friendship with my daughter, I can't let that happen unless I'm in the picture."

She ripped herself from my grasp. "So that's it? It's you and her or nothing?" Her laugh held all the sarcasm her next words accompanied. "I never once thought you'd play a game so low, Shane. Throwing away a promise you made me, little under a week ago, that no matter what happened between us, I'd never lose that daughter of yours. A beautiful girl I've grown to...to..."

"She loves her, son. Don't do this," Nora interrupted our discussion.

"Mom, stay out of this," I growled, pressing my thumb and forefinger against the bridge of my nose.

"This isn't the way to hold on to something you think you're losing," the older woman pointed out.

My body lost its rigidity, in its stead, defeat made me struggle to keep my legs beneath me. Looking up, my gaze met and held Emberlyn's and I just knew our conversation was going nowhere. Swallowing that ever-growing lump in my throat, I hoarsed out, "It doesn't matter, Mom, I already lost her. I'm willing to give her safety. Safety she's clearly taking because she's back here. She wants to help me solve the case. It doesn't matter that she's the first person since Eva I am able to see myself with, and be happy. Am I right, Emberlyn?" The last was spat as if the reality left a bitter taste in my mouth.

"W—what?" Emberlyn whispered.

"You heard me," I said, all too frustrated. Was she trying to gut me where I stood? "I'm fucking falling in love with you, and you can't even see it! Why do you think I lose my head when you go off and do something you damn well know you shouldn't? Why do you think I fought so fucking hard to have you here with us, instead of with Dalton or one of the other guys? Because I fucking care, alright? I care for you, dammit! I fucking fought my growing curiosity about you, until I couldn't take it anymore, after what my mother and daughter kept saying about you. I just had to know you. But I don't know you at all, do I? I—"

One second I was looking at a woman, whose face was buried between her palms, her head shaking from right to left, and the next, she'd knocked me clean onto my ass as she clung to me as though her life depended on it, her lips fused to mine.

I ripped my mouth from hers. "Em..."

Dainty fingers covered my lips to cease my words. "Shh." She peeled them back to deliver a soft peck, then replaced them. "I can see it, Shane. I hear you loud and clear." She punctuated each sentence with hard, but all too brief kisses before flooring me altogether. "And I've fallen. I—I'm still falling." Her eyes strayed to the side of my face. "But I'm fucking terrified."

My heart warmed, I felt powerful with just her words alone. I'd gotten through to her. Finally.

Cupping the side of her face, I brought her gaze back to mine, noticing my mother sneaking out of the kitchen to give us a moment.

*About time.*

"I'm terrified too, sweetheart. I'm terrified of losing my daughter...of losing my mom. I never thought I'd find something like this—*us*—ever again, so yeah...I'm fucking terrified of losing you too. But I can't live a life based on fear. And neither should you."

"That's a lot harder to do, Shane," she whispered.

"And that's why we should stick together," I said, offering her a soft smile, which she returned.

"Your daughter said something along those lines just yesterday, as a matter of fact."

"She did, did she?"

Emberlyn nodded. "She said I should stay because we were stronger as a team than when we're on our own."

"Bloody smart kid, that one," I chuckled.

She snorted. "A regular chip off her father's block, more like." Her face grew serious, and she stayed silent.

"Em, what's the matter?"

On a sigh, she dropped her forehead to mine and closed her eyes. "I wish I could keep this light feeling going, but I'm exhausted, and I need to talk to you before we go into the station, so I can give my report about the attack."

My own eyes closed as I took a deep breath.

I was pretty sure I wasn't going to enjoy any of what I was about to hear.


"What did he mean by, *you're not her*?" she asked me.

Emberlyn had just finished giving me the rundown on what her attacker had told her. It had been a huge point of contention in her decision to leave me in the dead of the night.

Still fuming, I growled, "He means Eva."

"Your wife?" I nodded. "Of course I'm not her."

"No, you're not," I bit out, "but it won't stop him from doing anything to get back at me." This just proved that the man was psychotic enough to stoop to any level to get back at me. For what, who the fuck knows; but I suspected jealousy.

The room was filled with silence for a few minutes before Emberlyn broke it.

"Shane?"

"Yeah," I sighed, rubbing the mounting stress off of my face before looking at her.

"I haven't been to the range since before I moved here. Do you think you could take me shooting sometime soon?"

If I couldn't let off steam by doing something physical, the range was usually where I found myself. It was as if she'd read me; or maybe she was finally coming to terms that running wasn't an option, but practicing with her weapon—a proactive stance—would provide her with the strength and added security she suddenly found herself lacking.

"Go," Mom interrupted us. "I'll look after Rosie."

"But we have that appointment at the station," Emberlyn stated.

"We can go before that. It shouldn't take us too long."

On a single nod, Emberlyn got to her feet. "Let me get changed, then we can head over to mine to collect my weapon."

You mean she didn't even have the fucking thing on her when she ran off? What the fuck was she thinking?

<h1 style="text-align:center">twenty-seven</h1>

Emberlyn

SHANE SEEMED LIGHTER SOMEHOW as we left the shooting range. When I'd asked him why, he'd simply told me that next to working out, it was a surefire way to get rid of his frustrations when things got tough.

I completely understood him. I felt more focused, in control, and stronger somehow—and maybe even a little hot under the collar. Having Shane show me better positioning to hit my mark a little easier had seemed important, but with his body pressed against mine, his arms surrounding me as he guided my grip, my stance, it ended up feeling a little like foreplay. Apparently, the loaded weapon in his pants thought so too as he'd pressed himself against my ass.

His, "You with a weapon, and knowing how to handle it, is fucking making me want to do things we definitely shouldn't be doing right here," comment, as we finished up by cleaning our respective guns, didn't help my case but sure as hell nailed the point home that he'd been feeling a little hot and bothered himself.

. . .

The looks I received from the front desk clerk at the station made me wish I'd taken Shane up on his back door entry option. I didn't need a look in the mirror before leaving the Peters' home to tell me that my eyes were black and blue, my nose was swollen and maroon, veering to purple-green in some areas. Add the crying I had done earlier, while both Shane and I had poured our hearts out to each other, and I knew things looked even worse. Puffier.

"Ms. Roth?" An older man in uniform approached us. Shane's hand squeezed mine in a reassuring manner that did nothing to calm my erratic heartbeat and the nausea churning in my stomach.

"Em, I'd like for you to meet Charles Dodge, my captain," Shane introduced.

I looked between both men, and only when Shane let go of my hand, with another reassuring squeeze and a nod to boot, did I put my hand forward to greet Shane's boss.

"Pleased to meet you, sir."

The man took a moment to size me up, a minuscule wince detectable when he got to my face.

"Trust me, the door did most of the damage over the man," I mused.

Apparently neither man thought I was funny by the sound of their groans.

*Do all cops sound the same?*

"Let me show you to the room we'll be taking your statement in." Captain Dodge swept his arm past him, toward a hall to his left. "Due to information which has come to light in an ongoing investigation, I've recused myself from my role in our Criminal Investigations Division and am helping out with our folks in Crime Prevention for the time being."

"Shouldn't be for too long, boss," Shane said, to which the man simply snorted.

"I can use a slight change of pace, Peters." The man eyed his former subordinate from the corner of his eye. "I'm thinking, after everything is said and done, I'm retiring."

I didn't miss the fact that the men seemed to be carrying a silent conversation with their eyes only they understood. I let them have it, despite my curiosity.

Reaching the tiny, clinical looking room, with not-so-white walls, I noticed three metal chairs and a small table which had seen better days. As we passed what must have been an observation window, Dodge stopped and gestured for us to precede him.

"Have a seat. Can I get you anything to drink before we start?"

My throat had suddenly run dry as soon as the man had mentioned refreshments.

"W—water, please," I croaked.

Nodding once, my soon-to-be interrogator disappeared around the edge of the doorway, leaving Shane and me alone.

"Are you okay?" he asked, as he pulled out a chair for me, then seated himself in the one next to it, grabbing hold of my hand.

All I could do was nod.

"There's nothing to be nervous about, sweetheart," he tried to assure me.

Of course there was! Shane Peters was merely hanging on by a thread at this point, I was sure of it. First, we'd had our emotional blowout. Second, I'd regaled him with the little delivery I'd received at that shitty motel I'd spent the night at. He'd actually surprised me by keeping his cool, but I knew he was fuming on the inside. Shane had simply asked to see the latest of my ex's deliveries, grabbed his cell and phoned it in to Dalton, also informing the man that he could call off the proverbial dogs from hunting me down. Dalton had only left him with one message for me: Devolin wanted me to call her within the next twenty-four hours. I'd promised Shane I would. There was no way I'd want that woman on my ass.

"I know you're not going to like what I have to say," I explained, averting my gaze from Shane, instead focusing it on our hands laying intertwined on my lap.

"I might not," he started, "in fact, I know I won't, because we've already discussed this, but it doesn't mean you can skip this part, Em." He tugged my hand to his mouth and buffed his lips over my knuckles. My eyes remained cast downward. "Would you rather I not be here when you give your statement?"

That made me look at him right quick. "Y—you'd do that?" He nodded, despite his discomfort with the idea clearly identifiable in his expression. This also served me with a reminder that the man led his life with transparency, truth, and full disclosure. He'd been an open book with me today.

And I owed him the same.

Taking a deep breath, I kept my eyes locked on his. "No..." I cleared my throat. "No, I don't want you to leave, Shane."

His relief was palpable.

"Let's get to it, shall we?" Dodge broke us from our conversation, dropping three water bottles in the middle of the table before he took his seat across the table from us.

SHANE

*Son of a bitch!*

The more Emberlyn recounted what had happened right outside her little cottage yesterday, the more incensed I became. It didn't matter that I'd heard the story beforehand because as I listened to it a second time, I was certain Casen Dodge was indeed my man. DNA put him at the scene, and he'd come and warned my woman off; that was enough for me.

The fucker was playing with me, and he was close.

A simple look in the captain's direction told me he suspected as much too.

"Can you tell me anything about him, Emberlyn?" Dodge asked.

She shook her head. "He smelled of body odor and old sour alcohol." Emberlyn closed her eyes. I recognized it as a gesture of effort to recreate the event—something many victims or relatives and friends of victims I'd interviewed in the past had done—and a ploy highly recommended by many psychologists and profilers in higher law enforcement agencies.

"Ember—"

Her body tensed and her hand grasped mine in a death grip, her nails digging into my palms.

"What?" I asked.

"He sounds just like you!" Her eyes snapped open and darted my way. I gave her a confused look. Casen sure as hell didn't sound like me. "Not you, Shane," she turned to face my captain, "*you.*"

Captain Dodge's eyes met mine and I nodded, then the man proceeded to get to his feet, extending his hand toward Emberlyn. "Ms. Roth," she reached out with a confused look, "I believe we have enough for the time being. If you can bear with me, I'll get these notes typed up in a report and will be right back for you to review it all. Once you sign off on your statement, pending no corrections, I'll let you get out of here."

"Okay," she whispered.

"And a side note," the older man paused at the door with a smirk on his face and a look of approval in Shane's direction, "next time, should you find yourself here for another statement, make sure to clean off the stink of the range. We wouldn't want anyone to get the wrong idea."

Half an hour later, Emberlyn had signed off on her statement.

We'd been in the car for all of five minutes when she said, "I want to help with your murder case."

Her words were so sudden—not so unexpected because

she'd voiced something about helping me when she'd come back this morning—that I stared at her, the car swerving violently.

"Shane, watch out!"

I corrected the car, pulling us back onto our side of the road, just as the driver of the vehicle in the oncoming lane laid onto his horn.

"What the fuck, Em!"

"Please hear me out," she begged.

"No," I argued.

"Shane—"

"I said no, Em!" My words were loud and hard enough to make her jump back in her seat. A few seconds passed before I realized I had been a jerk again. "Em," I started calmly.

Having gotten over her fearful reflex, she merely crossed her arms over her chest, jutted her chin out, and ignored me.

"Em," I tried again.

Her face tilted to stare out the passenger side window as she continued to disregard me.

*Fucking cute.*

Discussion unresolved, the final ten minutes of our drive home was spent in silence, but her constant ignoring only had me smirking through the windshield as I kept forward to our destination.

# twenty-eight

EMBERLYN

MEN WERE such infuriating creatures at times!

It wasn't enough that I was battered and bruised on the outside, but this morning's experience with giving my statement, and dealing with difficult questions about my attack, had left my brain feeling just as beaten down. And let's not get started on the morning's festivities that had rung me out entirely on the emotional spectrum.

Now, I had Shane reluctant to leave my side, say nothing for him questioning me incessantly about how I was doing; how I was feeling; what I wanted to do; if I wanted a drink...a blanket...lunch...blah...blah...blah.

It was nearing four, and Lana Rose was about to arrive home from school when I felt Shane's eyes on the side of my face. I just knew he was about to fire off another one of his stupid questions.

"Do—"

On a loud huff, I abruptly stood and turned, heading for the staircase, thus cutting him off before he'd had a chance to get his words out. Taking two steps at a time, I made it to the spare bedroom, then slammed the door.

I suppose my behavior might have been childish, but it sent a message that Shane would hopefully receive.

At about half past four, a soft knock sounded on my bedroom door.

"Come in." I sat up to greet my visitor.

"Ember?"

"Right here, sweets," I smiled, despite the slight twinge in the bridge of my nose from doing so. The best part of any day had just arrived. "How was your Monday at school?"

"Okay." She shuffled her feet, only having entered my room far enough to close the door behind her and that was it. "Where were you this morning? Daddy said you weren't feeling well and you were sleeping, but I know he lied."

She might have been nine, and her question was a tough one to answer. I should have known I was going to have to answer to more than just Shane and his mother. Lana Rose was no dumbnut.

"I—"

"I know because when I went to brush my teeth, I snuck in here and all of your stuff was gone."

*Oh no!*

That temper I'd seen so many times already from Shane was reappearing, but in his daughter's features, her words having bite to each of them as they came out.

When I didn't come up with an answer fast enough to her liking, she beat me to the punch.

"You ran away, didn't you?" The hurt in her eyes had shame filling me.

"Sweets, come here." I patted the edge of the bed beside me. "Will you let me say I'm sorry? I'll even explain why I did what I did."

"You will?" She looked surprised.

Nodding, I continued, "Of course."

"I thought you were going to tell me it was too complicated, and that I was too little to understand," she explained, as she hurried to my side.

"It is complicated," I told her, "but I think you're old enough to hear some stuff, especially because it involves all of us: you... me...your dad, and Grams too."

"Okay."


"So you left because you were scared?" Lana Rose asked. The girl was cuddled into my side; both my arms were wrapped around her.

"Yes, sweets," I whispered against her hair, then kissed it.

She pulled away slightly to look up at me. "Can I ask you something?"

"You can ask me anything, Rosie, you know that." I smiled reassuringly.

"Do you love me?"

My heart beat at a staccato. I had been leading us to this during our discussion, and this child before me had beaten me to the punch.

Pulling my arms from around her, I cupped her face, tilting it so she could see mine full-on. "With all of my heart, Lana Rose." She smiled, and I returned the sentiment. "You're kind of hard not to love, my dear girl."

"I love you too, Ember. You're my best friend, you know," she said so matter-of-factly. "Well, next to Daddy and Grams, of course." She giggled at the last.

This had me giggling along with her. "I suspected as much." I winked.

Then her expression went pensive as she bit down on her lower lip, signaling me that she had another question but wasn't quite sure if she should ask it.

"Come out with it, Rosie," I urged. "What else is eating at you?"

"If you love me, does that mean you love my daddy too? And what about Grams?"

The worry in her expressive face was comical, but the seriousness of her inquisition was more than enough to beat back any hilarity that may have manifested.

"Your grams is one of the best people I've ever known," I began, leaving the topic of her father for last. "She reminds me so much of my own mom."

"Where is your mom?"

"My mommy and daddy died when I was in college, Rosie," I explained.

Her little arms wrapped around me and squeezed. "So you're like me?"

Grief filled me as I hugged her back. I missed my folks something fierce right then. "Yes," I mumbled into her hair. "But I was lucky, sweets. I got to grow up knowing the very best parts of them both and seeing them every day until I was much older than you are now. They taught me how to take care of myself. I was in my very first apartment, and all grown-up, by the time I lost them."

"I bet you miss them lots, huh?"

"I do."

"I only remember Mommy because of pictures and what Grams and Daddy tell me about her," she told me.

Smiling, I said, "I bet you they've told you all of the best stories about her though, right?"

She nodded into my chest. "They do. All of the time. Daddy doesn't seem to run out of new stories."

*I bet.*

A man like him didn't strike me as someone that would miss regaling the daughter he adored with the best about the love of his life.

That thought left a sour taste in my mouth and a piercing sensation of insecurity in my chest that faded all too slowly.

Would he really ever be able to move on?


### SHANE


I'd been just about to knock on Emberlyn's bedroom door when I heard my name being mentioned.

"So you love me, you think Grams is something extra special...but what about Daddy?"

My fist dropped to my side, my feet shifted me sideways, then my body slumped quietly against the wall as I slid down it, my ass connecting with the floor.

"Rosie, I want you to know that no matter what happens with your daddy and me, I'll always love you."

"You're stalling, Ember." My daughter's whine had me smirking as I eavesdropped when I should have let the two finish having their moment.

"I just wanted to make sure you knew," Emberlyn said, humor lacing her words.

"I know, jeez!" I could only picture Lana Rose's signature eye roll, ready to bet that she'd delivered it with impressive apt.

"To answer your question...yes. I do love your daddy, sweets."

"Shane!" My mother's voice had me scrambling to my feet.

*Busted!*

# twenty-nine

**EMBERLYN**

SHANE?

Cutting our conversation short, I rushed to my room's door, only to find Shane and Nora facing each other in the hall in front of my doorway.

My eyes flitted between the two. Nora looked annoyed, her arms crossed over her chest with her eyes remaining on her son, while Shane looked guilty, a blush having filled his cheeks. For a short moment, I could picture a very much younger Shane, not much older than his own daughter now, being reprimanded by his mother.

Curbing the humor bubbling up inside, I focused on the present; loaning me with the seriousness needed in the moment. "You heard us, didn't you?"

"I did." Well, he didn't beat around the bush now, did he?

I huffed.

"Em—"

"I take it that dinner is ready?" I addressed my question to a now smirking Nora.

"That it is."

"Let me help you set the table." I turned to Lana Rose, who sported a beaming smile as she studied our interaction. "Come and help your grams and me, sweets."

Leaving Shane behind, we ladies headed down to the kitchen to put the finishing touches to our dinner.

## SHANE

Dinner had been a little awkward, to say the least.

While the ladies had chatted as if all was normal, I'd tried to engage Emberlyn in conversation—only to be ignored.

Repeatedly.

It burned my ass, but I knew it had a lot to do with my hovering over her like a mother hen all damn day.

*And maybe just a little with the way you outright refused her help before you'd heard her out.*

If there was one thing I remembered about my previous relationships—especially the one with my late wife—it was that when a woman said she wanted to be heard out, you sure as hell better listen.

It's a lesson I'd failed today.

"So…" my mother nudged my side as she washed the dishes and I dried, "what'd you do?"

I shrugged. "Too much in one day," I muttered, "but I'll make it right, even if I hate how I'll be doing it."

"That doesn't answer my question, Shane."

"I refused her help, before I even heard her out," I said, eyeing my mother from the corner of my eye, knowing I'd be witness to her disappointed headshake. "Then I treated her like a porcelain doll all afternoon, even though I know damn well she's strong and was dealing with the events of the last day entirely fine."

"So much like your father," she said, cupping the side of my face after having dried her hands on my tea towel.

"I just want her safe, Mom," I whispered. "I want all of you safe."

Her eyes shone with sadness. "I know, son, but you have to understand...a woman like Emberlyn...what she's been through—"

"You know?"

"Her grandmother had filled me in over the years," she said.

I nodded. "She's been hurt so much. She's had enough."

"She's tough, Shane. After what she's experienced, I suspect she needs to be in control of major decisions." She snorted. "She may not always make the right one—case in point, leaving you in the night—but that's something you both can work on if you want it to work out. Compromise, Shane. It's something you haven't had to do with a partner in years. Maybe if you learn to hear her out, you'd both be better equipped to make decisions that'll benefit the both of you."

I chuckled. "I think I've already figured that much out."

"There might still be hope for you yet, then," Mom said. "Your father never really clued in, God rest his soul. Oh, he let me think I had control at times, but I've always suspected he had a hidden motive that met his own wants in the end."

I grinned. It really did sound like Dad.

Grabbing hold of my mother's shoulders, I stared into her eyes. "Thanks, Mom."

"You're welcome." She smiled, then leaned up to kiss my cheek. "Now give me that towel and go make things right." Yanking the thing from my hand, she snapped it playfully at me once she'd stepped away.

Just as I was about to exit the kitchen, I turned and watched as my mother went back to her task, mumbling to herself in a satisfied fashion about sons needing their mothers to set them straight no matter how old they were.

Wasn't that the truth!

# *thirty*

**EMBERLYN**

DROWSY FROM SLEEP, the blurry vision of a man coming into my room had me bolting to a sitting position.

Had it not been for the bedside lamp still being on, I'm sure I would have been halfway to a coronary at this point.

"Shane?" I croaked, wiping the sleep out of my eyes.

"I have something for you," he whispered.

Looking at the bedside clock, it was just after midnight.

"Shane, it's late," I yawned. "Can't we do this tomorrow?" That's when I noticed the familiar looking file in his hand. Nodding to it, I asked, "What's that?"

"Something I believe you can help me with," he said, as he took a seat on the edge of the mattress next to my hip. "I spoke with Will, and we both agree we could use your help with that photomo...Whatever it is you said it was."

"Mosaic," I supplied.

"Yeah, that thing," he said, then licked his lips, his eyes boring into mine. "I'm sorry, Em. I'm sorry I didn't listen to what you had to say before shutting you down; and I'm even sorrier for treating you like you couldn't handle yourself after

142

we got back from the station. You did more than prove that you could at the range earlier." I took the file from him, dropped it on my bedside table, then reached for his hands. "You're so strong, but you've been doing it alone for so long that I simply wanted to be of use to you."

"Shane—"

"And I'm sorry for eavesdropping on you and Rosie too, even though I'm not really sorry I heard the end of that conversation, despite getting busted like a novice on his first case," he grinned.

It was so soon; maybe too soon, but after being overheard earlier, it's not like I couldn't fess up to my feelings. Hell, they'd become clearer during my talk with Lana Rose earlier, but the fact that he'd come to me—in the middle of the night—and was taking the help I wanted to hand out, without him knowing that *this* was exactly what I'd been offering to do for him...I was seeing things that much clearer.

*We're a team.*

Team.

Unit.

Family...

"I do," I croaked.

Shane's brows furrowed. "Huh?"

"Love you."

"I'm kind of easy to love, aren't I?" he smirked.

Snorting a short laugh, I playfully tried to smack him.

He blocked my efforts, gripping both my wrists before throwing his weight forward to force me onto my back, where he came to hover over me with that sure-of-himself grin of his.

"What's funny is I told Lana Rose the same thing earlier," I studied his expression, "that she was easy to love, I mean."

His eyes warmed. "You did?"

"Mm-hmm."

His grip squeezed my wrists as his face leaned forward. "Em?"

"Hmm?"

Lips rubbed lightly over mine before pulling back. "I..."

My lids had drifted shut when I thought he'd deepen his kiss, but when he didn't, I opened my eyes.

"For the record, I feel the same way."

His kiss may have stolen my breath, but his words sealed the deal and stole my heart; even if he didn't quite come out and say the exact words.

### SHANE

I woke to a warm body pressed up against my front, my arms wrapped around said form, one hand flat against satin skin, the other cupping a mound that all of a sudden had my mouth watering to taste.

"Morning," I whispered against the back of Emberlyn's neck.

"Indeed," she hushed, then attempted to move but I held her against me.

"Just like this, beautiful," I groaned, thrusting my hips against her rear so she knew what I meant. Immediately her breathing pattern changed. "Nice and slow."

"Please."

I released my cock by simply shifting my underwear down, using my upper thigh to part Emberlyn's. My fingers pulled aside the lace I loved seeing her wear so much, as her hand reached back to grab onto my length and guide me to her heat.

Once settled at her entrance, she let go, grabbed my hand, intertwining our fingers before bringing them up underneath her nightshirt. She proceeded to guide me through a sultry tutorial on how she wanted me to handle her cleavage as I thrust deep inside her.

. . .

As hard as it was, I'd left Emberlyn at home alone for my shift at the precinct. Pending any call-outs, tonight was going to be a long one—my first night shift in a month—and I hoped I'd be able to put a dent in the mountain of incident reports I should have cleared off my desk at least two weeks ago.

At eight, my cell rang, and I was glad for the small reprieve. Even more so when the caller ID announced that the call was coming from home.

"Daddy!" I heard as soon as I'd connected the call.

I smiled at her excited voice. "Hi, baby girl."

"Ugh...Dad!" she whined.

I cringed. "I don't think I'm ready to hear you call me that just yet." I could hear Emberlyn giggling in the background. "How was your day, honey?"

"Good. Miss Amelie said I was getting better at my multiplications, Maddie isn't friends with Sarah anymore, but she called me her bestie, and we started on our Christmas project!"

I chuckled. "Sounds like you had a long day."

"Uh-huh!" she paused. "Daddy, is it okay if Emberlyn and me have a sleepover tonight?"

"What about Grams?" I asked. Normally, when I went onto my night shift cycle, Mom would spend the first night *sleeping over* which meant they slept together in her bed.

"But Ember is our guest, Daddy. And Grams said she'd be okay so long as I give her the next one," she explained.

"It's okay with me so long as it's okay with Em."

"More than okay," she said. Obviously, the girls had me on speakerphone, which explained why Emberlyn's giggle had come through so clearly earlier.

"Did you brush your teeth...take your shower?" I asked, dutiful father and all that.

"I did. Ember let me use some of her special stuff too! I smell like flowers!"

My smile turned into a full grin, while parts of me shouldn't have reacted the way they did, the memory of Emberlyn's scent was far too strong to subdue those baser instincts of mine.

"So my bed'll smell like a beautiful garden?" I asked, shaking my libido's reaction to the side.

"Mm-hmm." I heard the two whispering in the background. "Daddy, Ember wants to talk to you. I'm going to go give Grams my goodnight kiss because Ember says it's bedtime."

"Good call. I love you, honey."

"Love you!"

The discernible click that told me that I was now off speaker was a sign that the phone was officially in Emberlyn's control.

"Hey, sweetheart," I husked on the line.

"Hey." Her voice came out breathy.

"Good day?" I inquired.

"Productive. I got a bit of work done for you. It's proving to be more difficult than I could imagine," she announced.

I groaned. "I wish you didn't have to do that. If I had it my way, I'd have you, Rosie, and Mom so far removed from this case."

She sighed. "I know, but do you really know of anyone else who knows the process in putting one of these together?"

I didn't, but that didn't mean Will and I couldn't have scoured various museums and galleries in the area to see if we could find someone who could. A specialist of some kind—did they even exist?

"You have to keep in mind that we don't have all of the pieces, sweetheart," I said.

"I'm not so sure of that," she told me. "We need to talk about what I've managed to get together. I think you might be closer to your man than you think."

She had no idea. I didn't talk about my ongoing investigations, so it was fair enough to say that Emberlyn wasn't privy to the fact we already knew who was behind these murders. The problem was getting our cuffs on the guy. She also didn't know we suspected her attacker had been one and the same as the murderer she was helping us catch.

"We'll talk some more about that tomorrow," I told her. "Right now, I want to know how you're doing."

"Tired." She yawned as she said this. "I think your daughter's homework wore me out more than it did her." Her voice carried a tone of happiness despite her exhaustion.

"I swear they seem to have more work than we ever did at their age," I stated.

"Yeah." A pause. "Listen, Rosie is barreling up the stairs, which means I should probably let you go and put her to bed."

"Yeah," I sighed.

"When will you be home?"

I smiled. "Miss me?"

"Only a little."

I harrumphed. "I miss you too, sweetheart. In any case, I should be home around four."

"Okay," she whispered. "Wake me when you get here? I want to know you're safe."

"I will." I'd have given anything to be with her and Lana Rose right then. "Sleep well, and give my baby a big wet kiss on the cheek for me, will ya?"

"I will. Goodnight, Shane."

"G'night."

Disconnecting the call, I saw I'd been on the line for near on fifteen minutes.

Yeah, it was going to be one fucking long night.

# *thirty-one*

EMBERLYN

WITH SHANE on the night shift over the last week, it was safe to say we rarely got to spend time together. Whenever we did, it was all about the photomosaic—the one I'd been all too excited to work on—also the one I'd incidentally begun to resent.

I'm not sure if it was the fact Shane and I had so little alone time together, or that when we did, Lana Rose was underfoot, but I was beginning to feel more like Shane's workhorse and live-in nanny—now that Nora was staying with an ailing friend for the next few weeks—more than his girlfriend.

Girlfriend.

Shit!

Come to think of it, we'd never really labeled what it was that we were, yet we'd smoothly coasted into a relationship that bordered closer to married and family life, than one with any kind of wooing.

Strong arms came to wrap around me, pulling my body into a warm hard one.

I wanted so badly to turn around and embrace the fact

Shane had come home early, but I was still nursing my snit. One he'd caused, and I'd told him so earlier when—like every night he'd worked this week—Lana Rose and I had called him to wish him a good night.

"I know you're awake," he whispered against the soft skin, right behind my ear. "Your body reacts to mine, even when you don't want it to."

*Dammit!*

"You're early," was all I could manage to say.

"You needed me," was his reply, to which I shrugged. "And for what it's worth, I felt the need to be here...with you." He gave me a squeeze. "I need you to turn around and look at me, sweetheart."

Fuck. I hadn't heard that pet name for most of the week. Realizing it just then, brought tears to my eyes, and before I knew it, I sniffled.

"Em?" I still hadn't moved. "My beautiful Em, please turn around so I can apologize properly."

I couldn't deny him when he was this sweet. So I turned in his arms and burrowed my face into his bare chest, wedging my arms between us. He immediately tightened his grip on me.

"I know I've been working you hard this week. I've thrown you straight into family life. You've been looking after my daughter, helping with homework, getting her off to school, cooking...cleaning. It's more than what you signed on for when we started seeing each other; and to boot, I've been treating you like one of my slaves for this case."

"I volunteered to look after Rosie when your mother told us her friend needed someone to help her out after her surgery," I mumbled against him.

He kissed the top of my head. "It still doesn't make it right. We haven't even been together for a month, yet you've jumped into playing mother and housewife."

I pulled my face back and tilted it to look up at him. "Shane—"

"Let me finish." His eyes stared deep into mine. "Sweetheart," his hand reached up to brush away a strand of hair that had fallen into my face, "if this is all too much, I understand if you want out. I don't want you to be here because of need. I want you to be here because you want to be."

"I do."

His lips pressed briefly against mine before he pulled away continuing, "I don't want to be your boss. I hate that you're working on this case, and quite frankly, your involvement has me freaking out because it's hitting too fucking close to home."

"Eva?" came spilling out of my mouth. When Shane's body grew taut, I knew my suspicions had been right. I'd seen far too many hushed conversations ending abruptly, as soon as I'd made my presence known, between mother and son, let alone one when Will, Shane's partner, had dropped in for an impromptu visit with a belated birthday gift for Lana Rose.

Shane took a deep breath, then relaxed. "What do you want to know?"

"She was one of his victims, wasn't she?" I blurted out. "I... couldn't help but notice how the victims all look alike." It hadn't been until my third night looking over Rosie that I'd noticed the similarities between the victims and Eva Peters.

"His first," he supplied, then tightened his grip on me as if he sensed my next thoughts.

He was obsessed with avenging his dead wife first and foremost.

*No wonder he's been treating me like a—*

"Don't even finish that thought," Shane commanded on a low growl. "You are not Eva."

"No...I'm not." I swallowed hard. Was he using me as a replacement for the wife he still loved?

"No, you don't understand," Shane argued. "You're *not* Eva, Em."

"I *know*, Shane." He was beginning to really piss me off.

"You don't look like her. You don't mother Rosie like she did. You don't act like her—"

"If you're trying to—"

"Stop interrupting me, Emberlyn." His mention of my full first name made me freeze; or maybe it was his tone that brokered no argument that did it.

"Then get to the fucking point so I can pack my shit and get out, *Shane*," I spat. "If all you needed was a babysitter, you could have just said so. I'd have gladly done the job."

Shane's jaw tightened, his lips thinning into a straight line. "I'm not saying any of this right." He sighed, then loosened his grip.

It didn't take me long to make my way out of his grasp, then out of his bed, reaching for the old flannel shirt of Shane's I'd adopted as my housecoat in the mornings. He sat on the edge of the bed, rubbing at his face in frustration before crossing his fingers behind his head in a defeated gesture.

"I'll go sleep in the spare room," I told him. "Stan called a few days ago and he's done with the alarm systems. I think it's best that for the next week, while you're still working nights, that Lana Rose comes and stays with me; that's if you still want me to look after her."

My hand was on the doorknob, and I had yet to hear any kind of refusal or agreement from the man. As the door pulled inward, silence was broken.

"You're more."

# *thirty-two*



## THANK GOD!

Two words. Apparently, that's what it took to make her stop and turn around to look at me.

"What?" she whispered, shutting the door, then leaning against it, forehead to the surface.

"You heard me, Em." Getting up, I headed toward her, stopping a step away from her. "She was a great mother, but you... you're the best friend Lana Rose never had. She confides in you, respects you. You make her smile the way I've never seen her smile before. Not even for me." I swallowed hard. "Yes, I still love my dead wife. She gave me the best of herself in our daughter, but the way I feel for her doesn't even compare to the way you make me feel."

"How is it that I make you feel, Shane?" her voice quivered.

"If I'm going to pour my heart out to you, at least please look at me," I said, feeling slightly annoyed that when things got serious, this wonderful yet complex woman seemed to resort to running.

Emberlyn turned to face me, despite not making eye contact.

*I'll take it.*

"When you smile, I feel it in here," I rubbed the middle of my chest. "Your laugh...makes me smile. When I'm the one to make you do that, my day is automatically better. Your touch calms me. Having you near makes life that much brighter, in a world so dark and gray thanks to what I do. You do everything you can to make my little girl's life easier, but what you don't get is that simply being around her makes her happy. You're a giver, a nurturer, a lover, and a protector." Her eyes finally came to meet mine. "You speak your mind. And even though you infuriate me to no end with certain impulsive reactions, I get why you do what you do. I hate arguing with you, but I love it all at the same time. You challenge me, and all of what I've said lists things I've always needed and never got with Eva. If she were to come back, I could never get from her what you give me. I don't want anyone else. I want you. You're perfect for me, Em... in every way, and that's the gist of it."

Reaching out, I grabbed onto her right hand and pulled her into me.

"I'm sorry," she whispered.

"So am I." I kissed her forehead. "Had I treated you the way you should have been treated, I doubt tonight would have happened. You're my woman first and foremost."

"Your woman, huh?" Humor laced her words, despite the weary look in her eyes.

"Girlfriend, woman, significant other...I don't care how anyone calls it, but let's face it for what it is. You're mine, Emberlyn Roth."

Her eyes closed as a peaceful look came over her face. "Yours," she mouthed, a small smile spreading over her delectable lips.

"Can I kiss you now?" I asked what I'd been dying to do since I'd first gotten home.

"Please," she breathed onto my lips right before she took charge.


### EMBERLYN

The following week had gone significantly better, even with relocating to my house. Despite the lack of one-on-one, Shane had become quite attentive. In spite of our opposite schedules, he never hesitated to show me affection, even when Lana Rose was around. If anything, he seemed to thrive on her reactions. It seemed the girl enjoyed her father's displays. To be honest, he doted on her about as much as he did on me.

As for the photomosaic, Shane had told me they'd discovered the identity of the murderer, and urged me to work on it, but at my leisure and not to stress to get it done. Imagine my surprise when I found out Shane's boss's son was the culprit. Let's just say that the web woven was highly tangled. Before Shane and Eva had become an item, it turns out that Casen and she had a past together. He'd disappeared for a while, only to turn up on the force—albeit as a traffic cop—at the same precinct Shane worked out of.

Today was Shane's last night shift before he had a full weekend off. I had prepped and delivered all of my week's orders before Lana Rose was due home yesterday, so I decided to spend my Friday working on the mosaic I had neglected for most of the week, but still had quite a bit left to fill in.

Sitting on my living room floor with far too many pieces remaining to place, I looked for inspiration on how best to organize them.

And I found it.

Staring back at me from my fireplace mantle was a framed shot of Lana Rose in her mother's arms. The same one that was on Rosie's bedside table—a shot that was far too familiar, and one that I had absolutely fallen in love with, so when the little girl had packed her bags, I'd brought it along with us and set it in a place of pride so everyone could see it.

My eyes darted down to the carpet, seeing far too clearly the distorted images as my hands began to work frantically placing pieces, maneuvering them around, repeating as often as I needed until an enlarged, partially complete, but distorted replica of that framed photo stared back at me.

Only one piece was missing.

*Shane mentioned something about him thinking it was some kind of a countdown.*

With dread making my stomach churn, I climbed up to my feet and rushed upstairs, barging into my bedroom where Shane was sleeping off his shift.

"Shane!" I panted as the man shot up in bed as if he was primed to take on a hidden attacker.

"What! What's going on?" The man's eyes were wild as he took in the room, settling on me.

"You said you suspected those pieces were part of a count-down or something, right?"

"Right."

"I think you need to see this." Without waiting for his reply, I ran back downstairs.

I could hear him stumbling to get his clothes on before his bare feet began to hit each tread.

"Where are you?" His voice was rough with sleep and most likely adrenaline.

"Living room," I told him. "Shane, you need to get to Lana Rose. I have a really bad feeling about this."

"I'll put Will on it." He grabbed his phone, holding his finger in a motion for silence to which I nodded. "Hey...Yeah. I need you to get to Rosie's school before it lets out. I think we might have a lead in the case...Thanks, man."

Phone disconnected, Shane's ass hit the edge of my couch while he stared down at the mosaic.

"Is there anything I can do?" I offered, doubting there would be.

"C'mere." He gestured with his hand, not looking at me. I did as he requested.

No sooner was I within reaching distance, he pulled me to stand between his legs and wrapped his arms around my waist, his head buried in my stomach. I fanned my fingers through his unruly hair, still mussed from sleep and tried to offer him comfort.

"I'm too close to this, Em," he rasped. "God, if I lose her too, I don't know what I'll do."

My heart broke for him and Nora. Hell, it broke for me.

"You can't think like that, Shane," I choked out. "Will's on his way to get her. He'll get there before she leaves. She'll be home soon."

# *thirty-three*



TRUE TO HER WORD, Lana Rose arrived at Emberlyn's fifteen minutes later.

"Daddy! Uncle Will let me ride in the front and turned the lights on in the cruiser," she announced at the same time, taking a running leap into my arms. I held her tightly and for much longer than my normal.

All this time, I'd been sitting on these pieces with only one missing. It scared the life out of me that Dodge could have struck where it hurt most at any point. Problem was, there was still one piece missing, which meant that someone else was going to get hurt before he came for me—unless that final piece was me.

Ten minutes later, I was still stuck in my thoughts. Emberlyn and Will were entertaining my daughter when Dalton showed up with a heavily pregnant Devolin and Brycen Matthews in tow.

. . .

Seeing as Emberlyn's house was decked to the nines with Stan's bells and whistles security-wise, I'd been okay with temporarily moving into her place. It would do a better job to keep the most precious people in my life safe.

"You need to let your mother know what's going on," Emberlyn whispered to me while the others sat around her dining room table, devising a plan of action, while Brycen typed away with Devolin at his side, giving him a run for his money.

"I will," I vowed, "but she'll be at Maggie's for at least another week." Emberlyn nodded, seemingly satisfied with my answer. After all, a hip replacement on a seventy-something woman took some time before said woman could do everything on her own again.

"I think I've got something," Devolin broke our tête-à-tête.

"What?" I got up, rushing to stand behind her, Dalton on one side, me on the other.

"I'm going to go check on Rosie," Emberlyn announced.

"Please." I gave her a meaningful look of appreciation. She'd been in Emberlyn's bedroom watching a movie, which should almost be over. The last thing I wanted was for her to come down and overhear something about the investigation which now included her.

### EMBERLYN

"You want to watch the next one with me?" Lana Rose asked.

I'd come to check on her, noticing she'd decimated the two slices of pizza we'd left her with from our earlier order.

"Sure." I propped a few extra pillows against my head-board, then kicked off my shoes before joining her on my bed. Lana Rose moved closer, cuddling into my side on a sigh, as we watched the end credits to the first of the *Hunger Games* trilogy.

"Is everything okay?" she asked.

"Everything is just fine, sweets," I reassured her, kissing the top of her head. "Daddy just needs help for some work stuff."

"He hugged me extra tight. Daddy doesn't do that unless he's been worried sick about me," she announced.

"Rosie, you'll have to talk to your dad about that." I wasn't sure how much he wanted his daughter to know, and I wasn't about to overstep my bounds.

"So something is wrong?" She arched her neck so she could look up at me.

"Yes and no," I simply stated, gaining a confused look from the nine-year-old.

Just then, the bedroom door creaked open.

"Mind if I join you, ladies?" Devolin pushed the door wider, revealing her large belly, which she was holding. "The guys kicked me out." My brows arched. Devolin didn't strike me as a pushover. "I'm having some Braxton Hicks contractions and Dalton wants me to take it easy," she explained on a grumble.

"You can sit next to me!" Rosie's smile beamed.

Next thing I knew, the movie mostly as background noise, Rosie proceeded with the grand inquisition—about babies.

In that moment, and with the topic the little girl and myself had been on prior to the other woman's interruption, I was extremely thankful to talk babies. So was Devolin, by the look on her face.

"I'd like a baby someday," Lana Rose said, breaking the peaceful silence. Turning to stare at the girl, I'd noticed she'd shifted just enough so that one of her hands rubbed Devolin's belly as it moved in subtle undulations when the baby shifted. Devolin had fallen asleep, and it looked like Rosie was fading quickly.

Shifting onto my side, I spooned her in a hug as I covered her rubbing hand. "Me too," I yawned. "Me too, sweets."

**S**HANE

"How did we miss this?" was the first thing I asked as soon as Emberlyn had disappeared. "Jesus Christ! He's been local this entire time?"

Dalton and Will were both on their phones. Dalton with Rex, one of our part-timers, while Will had our captain verifying the information.

According to what Devolin had managed to find, there was a property—albeit in a remote location on the outskirts of Jacksonville—that could potentially be used by Casen Dodge. Will was checking up to see if Captain knew anything about it.

Hanging up his phone, the man turned to me and shook his head.

"Cap says he'd heard of the place, but he had no idea it was still in the family. It's some old hunting shack in the bush that used to belong to his wife's father. She hated going up there, and since she was an only child, he assumed it must have been passed off to her in the will. He'd thought she'd sold it off years ago," Will explained. "She just told us she'd simply put the task on the backburner and over the years, had forgotten about it, until now."

"I need a unit sent out there," I told him.

"Cap's already taken care of that."

"I'm sending Rex and Cade in too," Dalton said, as he slid his finger across his phone's screen to disconnect the call he'd been on. "They're on their way now."

"ETA?" I asked.

"An hour, tops," he said.

"Good."


Will and Brycen had left about five minutes before, while I pulled out a beer, handing one to Dalton as we settled on the couch. The man needed it after his wife had managed to scare the daylights out of him with what seemed like severe Braxton Hicks contractions.

"She'll be fine, you know," I told him.

He sighed. "I fucking hope you're right."

"Eva had them bad when she was pregnant with Lana Rose," I said. "From six months on, if I remember correctly."

"Dev says it's normal. She's been through so much I can't help but worry, you know?"

"I know how it is." It was my turn to sigh, adding measure to my frustration by rubbing my face with a single palm. "Don't expect the worry to go away once this kid comes out though," I chuckled. "It gets worse."

The man groaned. "Yeah, I figured as much." He took a long pull from his bottle, finishing his beer off.

"I've been doing some thinking over these last few weeks," I started.

"Yeah?"

"Yeah." I paused. "With everything going on with this investigation, and with Em coming into our lives, I think it's time I make a few changes."

The man shifted in his seat, turning his body toward me, then leaned forward, grinning. "Any of those changes work to my benefit?"

My answer was simple—a nod.

"I'm glad to hear it, my friend."

"Good."

"So when's this change happening?"

"Let me see this case through to the end," I told him. "I'll be handing in my resignation before the ink dries on any of that closing paperwork. Timewise, I guess it'll depend on the captain and the bureaucrats."

"Keep me posted, brother. You know I'd have taken you on full-time over a year ago when NSI was finally in the black." He slapped me on the side of the shoulder as he got up. "Now that we're done for the night, let me get my wife and we'll get out of your hair."

That's when we found the most precious sight of all: three

beauties sound asleep, one heavy with child, while the other two protectively held her belly, all cocooned together.

"That's where it's at, right there, my man." Dalton patted my shoulder as he made his way past me and toward his wife.

He had no idea how right he was.

# *thirty-four*



THAT BITCH HAD MANAGED to figure it out. At least she was good for something. Who knew getting to Peters would end up being so easy.

*I guess that job at the pen worked out in my favor.*

I'd met Trevor Sykes while moonlighting for the Pender Correctional Center in Burgaw, North Carolina, three years ago. He'd apparently beaten his wife good, leaving her in the hospital within an inch of her life. Long story short, she put him in jail for a good long time, but the fucker must have gotten out on good behavior. Lord knew Pender was battling a fight against overcrowding, resulting in my latest ally's early release.

My gig as a security guard came right after Peters had put a nail in my professional coffin by reporting me for misconduct on some fucking burglary case which landed me into being a traffic cop. Of course, he hadn't been the only one to burn me that time; but rivers ran deep between that son of a bitch and me—back to before he'd first failed me in the academy. Truth of the matter was, he'd already broken the last straw years before that when he defaced what was mine. My Eva.

Eva was a beauty—no one else could hold a candle to her. It's why I'd gotten rid of them—those women.

*But you should have been more patient.*

Had I been, I could have gotten rid of that little shit of a kid she'd had with Peters, ridding her of him as well. Sure, it would have taken some time to gain her forgiveness, but that was Eva to the core: forgiving. It didn't matter what I did as we grew up together. She'd always take me back.

That incessant headache was back too; nagging me to do something about it. It usually entailed a special brand of therapy—a bloody one, but I would wait.

"Baby, come back to bed," the woman behind me begged.

She looked just like my Evie. Sounded like her too. But she wasn't; not really.

"I'm gonna go for a run," I told her. When my thoughts strayed to Eva Peters, it always left me repulsed by whatever woman I was with at the time.

She lifted her head and eyed the alarm clock. "At four in the morning?"

Ignoring her comment, I shoved my legs in my black sweatpants, then slid on my black hoodie, before making for the door. "Back in an hour, Liz."

The commotion around Emberlyn Roth's house over the last week had been almost comical. I'd been lying in wait, watching; especially when my grandfather's old hunting shack had been discovered. It was a fucking good thing I parked at a distance and made the rest of my way on foot. Had I used the old access road to get to the drive, I'd have been caught—no ifs, ands, or buts—what with the manpower floating around the place that night they'd come for me.

My skin began to prickle with the need to act, but I stayed put.

That's when I saw the man make his way around the bushes carrying something.

It wasn't until he was half a block away—having delivered a small parcel—that I made my approach.

"Sykes?" I asked, still not believing my luck at seeing him out of jail. The man was deranged. Maybe that's why we'd gotten along so well at the pen.

He stopped, turned around, and peered at me. His eyes widened with recognition. "Dodge? What the fuck are you doing here?"

"You're gonna get yourself into heaps of trouble, my man. We need to talk."

### SHANE

I was sitting at Emberlyn's kitchen island, nursing a cup of coffee, while the girls were puttering around in her cottage, staring at the pile of unopened mail that sat there when something caught my eye.

A bright red envelope stuck out of the pile.

Considering Christmas was around the corner, yet a month away, I thought it odd for a card to be arriving so early, but what did I know? I didn't send that shit out, which meant I never got anything either.

"What're you doing?" Emberlyn's voice knocked me out of my musings.

"Aren't you going to open your mail?"

"Why?"

"Because I've been here for a week and the pile seems to only be growing," I stated.

She smirked. "It's mostly junk anyway, but if it bothers you, why don't you just open it? Leave the bills and throw the junk."

That was all the incentive I needed.

I tore into the crimson envelope only for a tiny piece to come tumbling out of it onto the granite countertop.

Staring back at me were two words that chilled my blood.

*Time's up!*

## EMBERLYN

To say it was a chilly late morning was one thing, but when the frost bites you from the inside—thanks to another unwelcomed package—and continues to do so from the outside, long after you've retracted back into your home, that's when you know something's wrong.

I'd sensed it the minute I'd turned the deadbolts and reactivated my alarm. It was even more potent once I'd returned to the kitchen to find Shane inspecting something with the edge of the red envelope he'd grabbed, as soon as I'd given him permission to clear my mail.

"Shane?" I asked, my voice all too shaky for my own liking.

"Time's up," he muttered.

"What?"

"Time's up," he repeated on more of a growl. "That son of a bitch!" he roared, getting to his feet and stopping abruptly as soon as he saw what I was carrying. "Fuck me! Put the fucking thing down, Em."

He reached for his back pocket and hit a few buttons.

"D, we've got a huge fucking problem."

# *thirty-five*



**SHANE**

THE MOMENT I heard my daughter's blood curdling scream, I almost lost my mind.

"Rosie!" Emberlyn yelled out, the first to make a beeline for the back door leading to her little cottage.

I made one for the front door, my gut telling me she'd be there if someone had snatched her. Sure enough, after disarming the alarm system and unlocking the deadbolts, I swung the door open hard; not even registering the loud bang it made as it hit the inside wall, only to see some burly, disheveled, black-haired man shoving my daughter into the back of a black Toyota Sienna.

Gray eyes met dark ones. I would recognize them anywhere after having studied his mugshot one too many times: Trevor Sykes.

The stare-off lasted merely a few seconds, but they were precious seconds; time I didn't have and failed. In a short moment, Sykes was in the driver's seat and speeding off with the peeling of rubber.

Making a run for my vehicle, I yelled out to Emberlyn.

"Call Dalton and tell him what's happening. Tell him to get Will. Stay here and lock everything."

"Shane, no!"

"Your ex has my daughter, Em! There's no way I'm not going," I yelled from the open passenger window as I punched the gas.

I managed to stay with the tinted-out black van for a few miles, into the industrial part of Jacksonville, before Will motored past me in his cruiser, lights flashing, siren blaring.

My phone rang and I hit the hands-free button on my steering wheel to connect the call. "Yeah!"

"Go home, brother," Will ordered over the line. "The cavalry is behind you."

Just as he said it, more flashing lights appeared in my rearview mirror.

"I'm not bailing, Will. The fucker has my kid," I growled.

My blood boiled, and a cold sweat had broken out with the amount of adrenaline pumping through me.

"Peters, get your ass home," Captain Dodge's voice came loud and clear on the line. "That's an order, Detective."

"Ten-four, boss." The last thing I needed was a wrongful dismissal or a stint being watched and investigated by internal affairs if I didn't follow orders. Captain Dodge might have reassigned himself to another department, but he was still my superior.

As my foot let off the gas, and everyone passed me, I hoped I wouldn't regret my decision to back down.

### EMBERLYN

You know the saying *when it rains, it pours*? Well, apparently it rang true today of all days.

Devolin showed up with Dalton, who brought some guy named Rex, with a really angry scar running horizontally across his neck, even though his beard covered most of it. The man was seriously scary looking; and quiet.

Next thing I knew, I'd been asked to contact Nora, who was supposed to still be helping her friend, Maggie. When her phone went straight to voicemail, Devolin put her fingers to work and called up the information for one Margaret Wood. Imagine my surprise when Maggie—as the Peters called her—announced Nora had gone home earlier that day.

One look out the front window showed her car was parked in the driveway across the street, where it had previously always been.

I tried Nora's cell again, then the house phone to no avail. Then I tried a third time.

"Something's going on," I heard Devolin state exactly what I was thinking. I was about to agree with the woman when I heard the sound of fluid spilling right behind me, followed by a shrieked, "What the fuck?"

As I turned, I took in the scene of Devolin standing in the middle of a puddle, her shoes drenched, along with her pants. "Holy fuck!" came barreling out of my mouth at the same time Dalton rushed into the kitchen on a, "What the hell is going on?"

Rex wasn't too far behind, mumbling, "Oh shit!" as he grabbed his cell and began to punch in a series of numbers.

"Baby, are you okay?" Dalton was all over his wife.

"Beside feeling like I pissed myself, I'm fine, Kip, but shit just got real."

"The baby's coming." I kept staring at the puddle on the floor.

"Ambulance is ten minutes out," Rex announced.

"No need," Shane came racing into the room. "I'll drive you to the hospital. I can get you guys there faster."

"I got this," Dalton declared, even though the frantic look in his eyes told me he probably didn't have it as together as he claimed. "Right, baby? We've practiced this."

"I think I like Shane's idea more right now, Dalton," Devolin confessed.

"Let's go," Shane called out, turning to head out the door. Before I knew it, Dalton was hurrying Devolin out of the room, barely giving me a chance to give her a hug and wish her luck.

Turning to tackle some dishes in the sink, I was abruptly turned around to face Shane who smashed his lips to mine. "Cap sent me home," he growled, his features displaying his ire with that fact. "I'll tell you more about it when I'm done helping those two have a baby."

"Be safe," I whispered to the air where Shane had been.

# *thirty-six*

**EMBERLYN**

SITTING AT HOME, not knowing what was going on with anyone, was slowly driving me mad. Rex had gone over to Shane's mother's house, only to find the place locked tight and nothing seeming as though it was out of order.

*Maybe she'd gone for one of her long walks.* After all, she'd been cooped up indoors, looking after her friend for three weeks. That woman was normally hard to keep at home unless Lana Rose was there.

Lana Rose.

My beautiful girl. Yes, by now I'd mentally adopted the nine-year-old as my own. I could only imagine what was going through that child's head. Rage filled me the more I thought about Trevor. If I had one single moment alone with him, he was going to regret not staying away. As it was, I was sure that Shane would most likely be meting his own payback when he got his turn alone with him.

**TREVOR**

171

For the life of me, I had no idea why anyone wanted kids. The brat in the back hadn't stopped screaming and crying. The pitiful whimper only showed how weak the female species was.

"I thought I told you to shut up!" I hollered from my driver's seat.

I'd managed to get to my destination for a rendezvous with Dodge, but it had been a close call. Escaping one cruiser was one thing, getting away from three of them...miraculous is what I'd call it.

"What in the fuck does Casen want with you anyhow?" I questioned aloud.

"I—I need to p—pee," she stuttered.

"No can do."

A moment later, the pungent smell of urine filled my nostrils.

"Are you fucking kidding me?" I punched the steering wheel, careful to avoid the horn. Since we were inside some old car garage, I got out and slammed my door shut. Maybe if her father had slapped her around, she'd know how to listen. Storming to the side door of the van, I yanked the thing sideways on its glider and grabbed the kid by the front of her shirt. "You just couldn't hold it in, could you?" My eyes perused the old place, settling on what I'd been looking for. Throwing the runt onto the floor, I pointed in the direction of what I'd scoped out. "Bathroom's over there. Make it quick. You come right back, kid, or you won't like what I do next."

"Y—yes, sir," she whispered, then skittered off like the little cockroaches kids are, making her way to the john.

That's when I decided it was time to make a phone call. After all, why should Dodge have all the fun with this?


**SHANE**

If I'd had the time to see the humor in things, I'd have laughed my fool head off at Dalton's conduct, both prior and after arriving at the hospital. I've never seen a man come so undone at the sight of his wife like that. For anyone to have seen the sure and steady Dalton Kippers losing his cool, over the impending birth of his first child; it was definitely something to razz him about later.

I'd been pacing the waiting room for news on Devolin's labor progression—not to mention, more news on what was going on with the search of my daughter—when I heard a crackle over the radio Dalton had left with me.

*Finally.*

I'd been checking in with the guys repeatedly every fifteen minutes for news and had been met with absolutely nothing other than their *I'm working on it*s. My patience was running thin to the point I was about to snap.

"We have movement," Cade announced. "Looks like Sykes is looking for something. Seems a little unhinged and panicked to be honest."

"Got a bead on Rosie?" I asked.

"Nothing."

*Fuck!* Was it that hard to have proof of life?

Earlier, I was informed that JPD failed to stay on Sykes' van. Thanks to Brycen and Cade who were out there, they'd managed—barely—to keep up. Of course, it helped having an unmarked car over a police cruiser at times. The fucker had no idea he'd gained a tail.

"Got incoming," Brycen called out. "Silver F-150 just pulled up."

Just then my cell went off in my back pocket. My eyebrows scrunched up when I saw Emberlyn's number showing up.

"Em?" I answered.

"She escaped them, Shane!"

"What!" How could the guys have missed that?

"Rosie just called. She said they're in an old place that stinks of gas and other stinky stuff. She told me that there was one bad man and there were a bunch of cars and car parts all over," Emberlyn explained. "On her way to the bathroom, she saw the phone on the floor of the office."

One hand ran through my hair, grabbing the strands tightly. "Thank fuck. Is she okay?"

"I'm not sure, Shane."

"Is she still where he took her? You've got to tell me everything you got out of her, so I can tell the guys. Dalton's men managed to stay on Sykes. They've got a visual on him, but none of my baby."

"She's hiding inside. She mentioned a big pile of tires."

"Okay," I took a relieved breath. "Sweetheart, I'm going to hang up now. I have to relay everything you just told me to the guys."

"I'm going to find our girl, Shane," she announced.

"You stay put, Em, that's an order!"

"I can't."

"Em—"

"No, Shane! Trevor's got her because of me," she argued. "I'm ending this right now."

Before I could argue with her more, she hung up.

*Fuck!*

thirty-seven

Emberlyn

I KNEW I'd suffer Shane's wrath when all of this was said and done, but I had to do something when Trevor called my cell. I wasn't much surprised the man had found my number, despite my efforts to make sure he never found me. He had connections I couldn't begin to explain. He'd always been able to locate me, so having found my number wasn't anything new to me. Hell, he already knew where I lived—proof positive since he'd come for Lana Rose and had left all of those packages.

I hadn't imparted my intentions on anyone, but I planned to offer myself up so Lana Rose could be set free. Had I told Shane, or anyone at NSI, I knew they'd never let it happen, so I was going it alone.

It had taken a bit of convincing, seeing as Casen Dodge was the puppet master of Trevor's strings, or so it seemed. However, the lure of my ex getting his hands on me once more seemed too appealing to pass up for him, and he gave me the information I needed that Rex had refused to share with me when I overheard him on the phone with someone from NSI.

. . .

I was in my car, cringing as I drove through an undesirable neighborhood, goosebumps spreading over my skin. I looked for the old garage Trevor had told me he was holed up in. Five minutes later, I'd found it, parking in a spot that would be easy to escape from—if I were lucky enough to get out too.

Double-checking my purse for the weapon I'd stashed there, the same one Shane had perfected my ability to use only a few days ago, I allowed my anger to fuel my determination and began to make my way to the main entrance.

## CASEN

Control was slipping away and scrambling to regain it seemed useless.

I'd gotten into Peters' place, only to be interrupted by his mother coming back. I took care of the bitch with an old cast iron frying pan that was sitting on top of her stove. The woman never saw it coming. The small pool of blood that appeared under her head didn't leave me optimistic for a smooth recovery if she survived, should she be found, but it went a long way to quell my bloodlust for the time being. She wasn't the one I was after.

Scribbling a note for Shane to drive the blade home, should he end up living, I kept watch across the street at the comings and goings from Peters' latest piece of ass's home before making my escape.

It was time for me to put the second part of my plan in motion.

Things couldn't have gone better. I should have known Sykes would play into his urges to get his mitts on his old woman. What I hadn't expected was that he'd let Peters' brat escape.

"Find her," I ordered him.

"What the fuck do you think I've been doing for the past half hour?" he groaned, like the miserable whiny dog he was.

"Find her, or else I'll take care of your precious Emberlyn before you have a chance to do any damage."

That apparently worked.

As excitement riled the adrenaline in my blood, I couldn't help but grin. All was coming to a head, despite the few hiccups.

**SHANE**

The moment Emberlyn hung up on me, I knew I had to leave. The process of finding Dalton was eased when the man himself came my way, a big ol' smile on his face, which fell as soon as he spotted the rage on mine.

"Got to go," I told him. "Em went after Rosie."

"What the fuck? Where's Rex?"

"Apparently, she gave him the slip while he was making rounds around the house. He's still there and he's staying put. We've got Sykes's location. Another vehicle has showed up, and my daughter is somewhere in that area."

The man rubbed his palms down his face. "This is a massive clusterfuck." Pausing to size me up, he asked, "You sure you're okay to go, or do I need to go with you to keep you in check?"

"Stay with your wife, D. I've got this."

The man nodded. "Keep me posted." With that, I handed him his radio and hightailed it out of there.

Parking at the edge of the block, I chose to make the rest of my approach on foot. My phone buzzed in my pocket, and I whipped it out, knowing Cade and Brycen had made me.

"I'm going in," I stated.

"Meet up first," Brycen said. "There's a storage shack

behind the garage. Get there now. We've got two perps, your kid, and now your woman's in there."

"Why didn't you fuckers do anything to stop her?"

"Can't give ourselves away until we're sure we've got those men where we want them," he returned.

"Fine," I grunted. "But we're doing this my way."

"Roger that, boss."

I shook my head at the man's sarcasm. I'm sure one day he'd be paying for that mouth getting away from him.

# *thirty-eight*

EMBERLYN

THE PLACE WAS dark and dingy. Lights were turned off; the only clarity being loaned by the outdoor sun that tried to make its way through the dust and grime on each pane of glass in the place.

Everything was eerily silent until I crept up to the only door behind the front counter; at which point I could hear footsteps coming closer.

Weapon drawn, I made it far enough around the corner to tuck myself away, sight unseen, as some man with brown hair, and all-black jogging attire came out.

*That's not Trevor.*

Outnumbered.

With both men on premises, I would surely lose any physical battle; but the need to get to Lana Rose, removing her from certain danger was driving me.

As soon as the stranger's shadow disappeared around the corner, I made my move toward the back.

. . .

If I thought the front end of the deserted shop was freaky, the back was even worse. There were various piles of tires, all in front of the bay doors that once allowed for cars to drive in and out for servicing. As Lana Rose had told me, there were a couple of cars, each in a state of disassembly, and piles of car parts strewn everywhere. The place looked as if whoever had once owned it had simply upped and left without trying to take anything with them.

Crouching low behind the pile of crap closest to my point of entry, I tried to see if I could find the hallway with the restroom Shane's daughter had gone toward. My guess would be she wouldn't have strayed too far from there for a hiding spot.

The slamming of a door made me jump.

"Where the fuck is she?" a familiar voice demanded. "Her car's on the lot."

*Holy shit, that's him!* The familiar voice belonged to my attacker, which meant...

I attempted to creep closer, staying concealed behind pile after pile, so I could hear their conversation better. Okay, so I was perhaps hoping to maybe find Rosie without coming out of hiding, so we could both get the hell out of there.

In my efforts, my foot caught on the edge of a muffler, sending a few old parts scattering to the cement flooring, which generated a loud clang.

"Ah, there she is!" the stranger announced. "Emberlyn, come out, come out, wherever you are."

His cajoling tone alluded to his craziness, sending shivers down my spine and chilling my blood.

"I'd do what he says, Emmie." This from Trevor.

Realizing I had no choice, I tucked my gun under the front of my shirt, glad I'd chosen to wear something a little looser in fit today, and got to my feet slowly.

"Where is she?" I croaked, my throat having gone dry.

"That's what I'd like to know," the stranger stated.

"Relax, Dodge, I have her in the side office," he said.

"Dodge?" came flying out of my mouth. "As in—"

The man smirked. "I see my reputation precedes me."

"You're a murderer," I declared. "You've killed...all those women." I gulped. "Eva."

"Don't you dare speak her name!" he bellowed, taking a few steps toward me until Trevor put a stop to his movement.

"You promised she was mine," he growled.

Goosebumps spread over my skin as an impending sense of doom filled my senses. He'd killed Eva and fifteen others, what said that he wouldn't be doing the same to Lana Rose and myself?

*Fuck my life!*

### SHANE

"She's in there, Shane," Cade told me. "Both of them are. We have fire, but the last thing we want to do is go in, guns blazing."

"Don't need that," I said shortly. "You've got me. It's what the fucker wants. Hell, it's probably what Sykes wants too. Me... dead."

"You're not going in there by yourself," Brycen said with finality.

"Then what are our options? This isn't a hostage negotiation scenario. This is personal, guys." I sighed, pacing a few steps away, then back again.

Cade, a man who showed emotion rarely, grinned. "Listen, I think I know how we can do this."

By the time Cade had finished explaining his detailed plan, a few more of the team had shown. Surprisingly, Dalton had done the exact opposite of what I'd told him to and had come along, having picked up Rex on his way.

"Before you lay into me for deserting my wife, she's the one who told me to get my ass out here," Dalton explained.

I nodded, then turned to Cade with a conniving smirk. "I think your plan needs a bit of a revision." The more men we had on task, the better off we would be.

Cade and Brycen were on exit points, while Rex guarded the front, Dalton and I taking the lead and going in by the main entrance, which we'd cleared a few minutes earlier.

"Find your daughter, then let me handle the fuckers and get your woman out," Dalton reiterated the agreed upon plan. "I want this to go smoothly, no going off half-cocked."

"We're good, D."

"Good. Let's go."

Clearing the door to the back, without being noticed by anyone on the other side of the door was going to be interesting, but oddly enough, when we got to the other side, no one was around.

"Ember!" Lana Rose cried out.

"Let her go!" Emberlyn cried, tears distinct in her voice. "You told me you'd trade, Trevor. So be a man for once in your life and live up to your fucking word."

*That's my girl.* No matter what, though, her ass would be meeting the flat of my palm when this was said and done. It took everything in me not to make a mad dash, but I'd be putting too much at risk, so I clenched my jaw and stayed put.

"They're not going anywhere," Casen Dodge's voice was hardly recognizable.

Peering at Dalton, who looked as if he were ready to explode, he signaled me that we were on the move toward the voices. Weapons drawn, we crept toward the commotion which was coming from down a hallway, right around the corner from where we were positioned.

"You can have the kid, but she's mine," another man—I figured to be Trevor—stated. "You promised."

"I promised nothing, Sykes, but don't worry, I'll let you have your fill after I'm done with her."

"Get away from me!" Emberlyn shouted.

Dodge tsked. "Oh, Emberlyn, I only want to play." Such a patronizing tone. "You'll be glad to know it isn't you that I want. You're not my type."

"Oh, I know who your type is, asshole," she growled.

A hard snap of skin on skin resounded. "Shut up, bitch!" A piercing scream from my daughter came next. "But you, my little Evie, you I could have even more fun with."

The urge to storm in there and take Dodge and Sykes out was about to take over. So much so that Dalton sensed it and had to restrain my forward movement. I'd had no idea I had already been moving toward the chaos I was blindly listening in on.

"Get away from her!" Emberlyn ordered once more as Lana Rose yelled out, "Mommy, he's got a knife!"

One look at Dalton told me all I had to know. We were going in.

# thirty-nine

**EMBERLYN**

ONE MINUTE I was flying through the air at my intended target, and the next, I was on the floor, searing pain radiating in my side, while chaos hit at full strength in the small room. Bullets were flying, yet I didn't recall seeing any other guns, other than the one I now remembered was still tucked into my pants. It was useless anyway, considering I could feel the lights dimming, my eyes growing heavy.

Grunts, fists against flesh...hisses and the coppery smell of blood filled my nostrils.

Then nothing...

Disoriented was one way of putting it. Consciousness regained, I kept my eyes closed until I heard a disgusting crunch of what my only guess was bones breaking and a man wailing.

"S—she was mine, first," came sputtered.

"I'll ask again," I recognized Shane's growled voice. "Why?"

"She was mine l—last," Casen's teeth chattered.

With another sickening crunch, my stomach wanted to revolt.

"I should eviscerate you like you've done to those women."

"It won't change a thing," Casen said. Fist against flesh resounded in the air, followed by spitting and very low laughing. "I would know. The lure of the spilt blood only gets stronger. You'll come to see it in time."

Oh dear God, this guy was sick. No sane person could get their jollies by harming another human being.

"I'm done," Shane declared, and in the next second, my eyes snapped open simultaneously with a gun going off.

SHANE

It was over.

Lana Rose was safe.

Emberlyn—my heart ached—was safe but would need medical attention. She'd hit that floor pretty damn hard.

And Casen Dodge was no more.

Staring at the brain matter spattered all over the office space, I was brought back to the present when a hand grasped my ankle. My first instinct was to kick out at the son of a bitch that was trying to get to me, but my mind snapped my reasoning into focus so fast, I'd realized that there was no more danger.

Peering downward, I took in the pale form of the woman I loved with my whole heart. Thank fuck Dalton had made away with Lana Rose when he did. Suffice it to say, our plan hadn't worked out the way we'd intended it to, but we'd come out on top, albeit a little banged up.

"Rosie," she whispered.

The one word had me collapsing onto the floor beside her, brushing the hair out of her face. "She's safe," I told her.

A sigh escaped from her lips as her eyes closed, her lips forming a grimace. "I think I might need an ambulance."

It wasn't until I inspected her more closely that I noticed the large gaping gash on her side, right below her ribcage.

"Oh fuck," I said, my voice hoarse. Putting pressure on her wound with one hand, I reached into my back pocket for my phone. My hand, barely able to function from the slew of punches I'd thrown at Dodge earlier, made things difficult to dial 911.

"911, what is your emergency?"

"My girlfriend's been stabbed. I think her lung may be punctured," I explained. "She's not breathing right."

"Okay, sir. I need an address." I provided it. "Stay on the line until the medics get there."

Dropping my phone to the floor, I leaned down into Emberlyn's face. "Stay with me, sweetheart. Please stay with me."

"Always," she whispered, then her body went entirely limp.


"Will she be okay?" Lana Rose asked as I found myself in the hospital waiting room for the second time today.

"The paramedic seemed to think so," I answered. I hoped the man had been right on that front. By the time we'd reached the hospital, Emberlyn had looked as white as a ghost from the loss of blood that had surrounded us on that disgusting garage office floor. They'd suspected internal bleeding was the culprit.

The waiting room was filling up quickly with everyone we knew: Rex, Cade, Brycen, Will, Captain Dodge, and a few other guys from the precinct. Dalton was here too, but he was going between floors to spend time with Devolin and their new baby boy, Carter. I'd even seen Skylar, Dalton's sister, pop by; then again, she did work here.

"Any news from your mom?" Brycen asked.

That was another thing that bothered me—her lack of contact after numerous attempts to get in touch with her.

I shook my head to indicate the negative. "I want to send someone over to the house to take a look inside," I told him.

"I'll go," he volunteered.

Removing my house key from its ring, I handed it to Brycen. "Thanks, man."

"No problem."

An hour later, a nurse approached us to let us know that Emberlyn was out of surgery. It turned out the knife she'd been stabbed with had nicked an artery, and the bleeding had ended up pooling into her chest cavity, compressing her lungs.

She'd be sore as hell, and she'd have to work on breath training for the next little while, but she'd be fine.

"Can my daddy and I see her?" Lana Rose asked.

The nurse eyed me suspiciously, then turned to my daughter before crouching down to her level.

"And who might you be to her?"

"She's my mommy," she stated plainly.

This was the second time I'd heard her say this about Emberlyn, and it warmed me to the core, despite leaving me feeling a little sad. All of this time, I knew she'd been searching for a mother figure, and I'd denied her. It made me wish that found Em a lot sooner. Then again, I had; I just had been too caught up with work and vengeance I couldn't see past those things for the gem my mother and daughter had discovered.

A tug on my hand and a, "Come on, Daddy," had me snapping out of my musings.

Following the nurse, I wasn't quite sure what to expect when we reached Emberlyn's room except, what I did see, had me cursing a blue streak a mile wide.

<h1 style="text-align:center">forty</h1>

EMBERLYN

THE CONSTANT BEEPING was what woke me. I shifted to turn the bloody alarm off, only to be met with excruciating pain in my side and a gentle hand preventing me from moving further.

"Don't move, Ember," I heard a female voice say. "You're alive. You're in the hospital with a chest tube in your side, to drain the fluid that built up inside of you."

"Do...do I know you?" I asked, after cracking my eyes open. The woman looked familiar, but my head was so fuzzy, I wasn't sure if it was a temporary memory block, or if this person and I had actually met.

The woman gave me a kind smile, and that's when I noticed her scrubs. "You're...nurse," I slurred.

"Dalton sent me in here because he trusts I know my shit, and he had to help Shane with something," she explained. "I'm Skylar, D's sister."

Skylar—Devolin had mentioned something about a Skylar a few times in our conversations.

"You're Devolin's best friend, right?"

"That's right," she beamed. "And I'm officially an auntie as of today, too!"

"She had the baby?" The heart monitor was beeping frantically with the quickening of my pulse. "What did she have?"

"A boy. Carter."

I closed my eyes, feeling my lips tug upward. "Carter," I whispered, thanking the higher powers above that some good could come of this day. The thought of kids brought Lana Rose to mind. "Fuck...Rosie."

"That sweet little thing is just fine," she patted my hand.

"Dodge?"

"Dead."

"Trevor?"

I got no answer, but with the way the woman beside me was biting her bottom lip, I knew that none of what had been happening was completely over.

"It's not over," I verbalized my thought.

"You'll have to talk to Shane or Dalton about that," she answered. "I'm not privy to my brother's cases, unless he shares, or I happen to overhear something. My brother is a vault when it comes to his business."

I gave her a curt nod. "Okay."

"You need to rest. If you're lucky, the doctor will be here in the next few hours to see if that tube is ready to come out. Trust me on this, it's not a fun process."

I cringed. "Thanks for the heads-up." My sarcasm was potent.

### SHANE

How could a day go from bad to worse, to better, then reach the pits of hell? When my phone rang, listing Brycen as the caller, the sinking in the pit of my stomach told me all I needed to know.

If Mom had been all right, she'd have been the one to call; but she wasn't.

"Shane...fuck," the man sounded torn up as I left Lana Rose at Emberlyn's bedside and exited her room. "It's your mom, man. I found her. The paramedics are working on her before they can get her a transport to the hospital."

"What?" My breath left me in a whoosh. I took the necessary few steps back so I could let myself fall into a chair.

"She's been messed up bad, Shane. Frying pan," he explained. "Massive blow to the head. There's a note here, I've taken pics of it, but it's from Dodge."

"I don't care what it says right now," I growled. "The fucker is dead, just text it to me, but please tell me she'll be okay." My phone went off with a notification; the man had done just as I'd requested.

"I don't know." His voice was filled with sorrow. "I'm sorry, bro. There was a lot of blood loss, and because I'm not family, the medics won't talk to me much." I heard a shuffling in the background before Brycen spoke up. "They're loading her up and heading out. I should be there in fifteen."

"Right." My voice shook.

"I'm sorry, Shane."

"Yeah. You've said that already," I said dryly. "It's not your fault. It's mine."

"Shane—"

"See you soon." Without waiting for a reply, I disconnected the call, letting my arm fall to my lap as I pulled up the image Brycen had sent over.

*I killed your wife.*
*I did your mom too.*
*Next is your daughter, then I'm coming for you.*
*-CD*

"What's up?" Cade walked up and asked, having noticed that something was wrong.

"I—I need someone to look after Rosie," I croaked.

"You've got it," the man said. "Anything you need, it's yours."

"Dodge hit up my mom's place this morning. She's been home all this time, probably hemorrhaging out of her brain," I growled low. I didn't need my daughter overhearing me, and freaking out about her grams when she had more than enough to deal with between her kidnapping and seeing some of the violent parts of what went on with her rescue.

"Fuck," the man grumbled, scrubbing at the scruff of his chin.

"I'm fucking sorry, man," Rex grunted. "I've really fucked up today."

Our eyes met. "Rex, if anyone fucked up, it was me. You did what was asked of you. I should have made certain all was right by sending someone in and not taken the fact the doors were locked as if shit was fine."

"Yeah, but it doesn't take the sting out from not being able to manage to keep your woman from getting into trouble," he rebutted.

"Trust me, Em has a talent for getting into trouble," I told him. "Her big heart makes sure of that."

The guy chuckled without much humor. "Yeah...most women do have the knack for finding it; you'd think I'd have clued into this by now." A flicker of darkness passed through his eyes, and not for the first time, I wondered if he spoke of experience. Something told me yes.

*forty-one*

THE NEXT TIME I AWOKE, I heard the snick of the door to my room shut. Tilting my head to see who'd come in, I was met with Shane's red-rimmed eyes.

"Shane," I whispered.

His eyes filled, tears spilling over as he came to my side.

"I'm sorry, sweetheart," his voice shook. "Fuck, am I a sorry fucker."

"Honey..." I let my voice trail while I lifted a hand to cup the side of his face as he bent forward so I could reach him better. In that moment, I saw everything he was feeling. My eyes welled up; my chest tightened. "Shane, I'm okay. Rosie is okay. Everything is over now."

He shook his head, pressing his cheek deeper into my palm. "He got to Mom," he choked out. "We're not sure if she's going to make it. She's in surgery now, but it looks bad, sweetheart."

Silent tears fled my eyes and drifted down my cheeks. "Where's Rosie, Shane? Does she know about her grams?"

He shook his head, no. "I can't do that to her. Not yet. She's been through too much already, Em." His entire body shuddered as he tried to stifle his sobs.

"She'll pull through, Shane," I tried to reassure him as much as myself. "She just has to. Nora is too stubborn to give up."

"They said she'd been lying there unconscious for a while, Em."

"Some people have been through worse, Shane. I need you... Rosie needs you to be positive on this one. I just found my family. I'm not losing anyone just yet and that includes your mother." My voice had gotten stronger with each word, taking my breath and a whole lot more energy along with it, but it had needed to be said.

"Okay, sweetheart."

"Knock, knock!" Cade peeked his head through the crack in the door. "Someone would like to make sure a certain special someone is okay."

"Please." I forced a smile, taking back my hand and wiping at the tear streaks on my face. I needed to be strong too.

As soon as I was done, Shane claimed my hand in his tight grip. "Send our baby in, Cade."

The man nodded, then disappeared.

"Ember!" Lana Rose exclaimed as she came in. I could see the excitement in her eyes, but her composure was one filled with hesitancy.

"Come here, sweets," I gave her a reassuring smile.

She came to perch herself on Shane's knee, reaching out with both hands, enveloping both of ours in them.

"I was so worried," she whispered, tears welling in her eyes.

"Me too, Rosie, me too." I gave her a solemn look. "I'm sorry you had to go through what happened today; but I'm so very proud of how tough you were."

She looked at her father, smiling a grin of pride. "I was tough. Just like Daddy."

"And smart too," I added. "I don't think I would have

thought to find a phone and call someone for help. That took a lot of guts. You're so brave, my girl."

She simply nodded, then cuddled into Shane. "When can we all go home?" she yawned, the day clearly leaving its mark on the tiny spitfire's energy reserves.

Shane's eyes met mine, as though telling me he wasn't leaving my side until I was released from the hospital.

"You need to take her home, Shane."

Lana Rose lifted her head from her father's shoulder and looked at me questioningly. "Aren't you coming?"

"I can't, sweets. I'll be in here for at least a couple of days, I think. I'm not sure, really, because I haven't seen the doctor yet," I told her.

"Then I'm not leaving." Crossing her arms over her chest, she jutted her chin out in classic stubbornness, as though that was the end of the conversation.


### SHANE


Mom made it through surgery, but they'd had to induce a coma for at least the next week due to the substantial amount of brain swelling.

The doctor had warned me she wasn't quite out of the woods yet. Due to the complications that came from lack of immediate treatment, it was quite possible she could suffer from secondary bleeds. There was also the fact that once they ceased using the barbiturates which kept her under, that she may not wake up on her own. Basically, despite the surgeon's optimism, it was a waiting game.

Returning to Emberlyn's room, my heart stilled when I took in the sight that greeted me.

"You shouldn't be up there, baby girl," I whispered, seeing as the woman presently cuddling my daughter was sleeping.

"If it makes you feel better, she actually told me no, until I told her I wasn't sure if I wouldn't have a nightmare," Emberlyn surprised us all.

I smirked. "Sweetheart…"

She never opened her eyes, but a small smile spread itself onto her face. "I need the cuddles, Shane, and you're too big for this bed. Besides, she's on the side I have nothing on, so we're safe."

"I'd give you anything, you know that, right?" I whispered, running my fingers gingerly over the hair at the top of her head in a soothing manner.

Her eyes crept open slightly. "Mmm. Tempting me, Detective Peters? If you're not careful, I'll make you break us out of this place. This bed is hard as a rock."

I chuckled. "I'd do anything but that, sweetheart. You're here until the doc says you can go."

She sighed, squeezing Rosie's shoulder. "Fine."

"Okay," I said.

"Sleep, now, Mommy," Lana Rose whispered.

Third was definitely a charm. I watched as a peaceful smile spread on Emberlyn's face, a single tear escaping the corner of her eye.

Christ, my girls undid me.

# forty-two



IT TOOK another day and night in the hospital before Emberlyn was finally released. That day had been a joyful one, because normalcy was slowly reintegrating itself into our everyday lives. Unfortunately, my mother was still in her induced coma, but healing well, according to the health professionals I spoke with.

With everything that had happened, I'd put in for a sabbatical from the JPD—one Captain Dodge was all too willing to provide. Despite having a murderer for a son, he still had a hard time digesting the fact that his one and only child was now dead.

That first night in Emberlyn's house had been a dream. With Lana Rose upstairs in the guest bedroom she'd started personalizing with my woman's permission, we found ourselves in bed early, cuddled with one another as we watched mindless television.

"I know it hasn't been that long, but I missed this," she whispered against my bare chest, her breath tickling as it slid over my skin.

"I missed this too, sweetheart." I kissed the crown of her head. "Are you comfortable?"

She lifted her head slightly to look up at me. "Are you kidding me? Anything better than this would be a cloud. That hospital bed did more harm than good, honey."

I chuckled. "I'll see about straightening out those kinks when the time is right, how's that?"

"Mmm...I'll look forward to it."

The next morning, I woke up to profuse swearing. Upon opening my eyes, I saw a sprawled-out Emberlyn on the floor.

"Fucking men!" she uttered.

"Hey now, you just woke me up, so what could I have possibly done wrong already?" I smirked.

Apparently that was a bad move.

"Clean up your fucking shit!" she stated. "I just tripped on your shoes, jerk."

Worry hit me immediately and I jumped out of bed. "Shit, Em! Are you okay?"

"Aside from having an already bummed toe, and stitches holding my insides together, I'm just peachy," she growled. "What's another few more bruises, right?"

"Sweetheart, I'm sorry," I came to crouch low beside her, helping her up to her feet. That's when I saw the small stain of blood on the side of her shirt. "Shit."

"What now?" she grumped.

I hurriedly pulled at her shirt, lifting it clean off of her, to reveal a fully nude upper torso. "I need to look at your stitches. I think you might have torn them open." I all but dragged her toward the bathroom adjoining her room. "Sit."

I turned to the cabinet and grabbed the stack of facecloths I had yet to put away from my stint of laundry yesterday afternoon. Wetting one, I turned to find Emberlyn inspecting her side.

"Let me," I said, kneeling in front of her and gently removing the gauze that covered her wound.

Dabbing at her side, I inspected the wound closely. "Looks okay," I whispered. "The stitches are fine. I think you might have just opened up the wound a bit. Let me get some of that ointment and a new bandage, and I'll finish patching you up."

She nodded, all the while following each and every one of my movements.

When I was done, I bent closer and kissed the top of her bandage lightly. "There, all better."

Emberlyn's hand reached up to cup my cheek, and our eyes met and held. "Move in with me," she whispered.

"What?"

"This morning proves you're all but officially living here, and you're clearly feeling at home if you're doing laundry, cooking, and cleaning. Hell, you leave your stuff lying around everywhere. You might as well have all of your stuff here," she all but blurted.

I swallowed hard. "Are you sure?"

"Does that mean you want to?"

I grinned. "Sweetheart, I'm a thirty-seven-year-old widower with a nine-year-old kid. I wasn't exactly looking to keep living with my mother for the rest of my life."

Her grin matched mine. "Is that a yes?"

"Fuck yeah, that's a yes." Cupping her face in my hands, I pressed our foreheads together. "In case you missed it—and I'm sure you didn't—Rosie thinks of you as her mother. So long as she's okay with it, then it's a go."

"Good," she smiled, "now kiss me to seal the deal, then go and clean up your fucking clothes."

Laughing that hard first thing in the morning was a foreign thing for me. It fucking felt awesome.

**EMBERLYN**

"Would you just stop it already? It's not like the Queen of England is coming for breakfast, Em, you're feeding my daughter...something you've done countless times already." Shane laughed.

"I can't help it," I whisper-whined. "I want her to say yes."

"Sweetheart." He came to a stop behind me, confiscating my spatula and wrapping his extra arm around my stomach, careful not to put pressure on my wound. "She loves you, of course she'll say yes."

I let go of the large breath I'd been holding onto. "I love you."

"I love you too, Em."

"And I love the smell of pancakes in the morning!" Lana Rose called out as she bounced into the kitchen.

"Have a seat, baby girl, we need to talk to you." Shane sure as hell wasn't going to beat around the bush by the looks of things. "Em, sit down. I'll serve us up." With a quick peck to my lips, he patted my butt in a playful manner, urging me toward the breakfast table.

"Sweets," I began, "how would you feel about you and your dad moving in here?"

The girl looked confused. "Is Grams coming too?"

I smiled, but Shane took over. "No, honey." He grabbed my hand. "After everything we've been through, Em and I would like to make us a whole family. I thought we'd have our own house by now, but it was so much easier to just stay with Grams, all these years, and help each other out."

"I want you to be my little girl, Rosie," I told her. "I love you, and I love your daddy, and nothing would make me happier than if you both came to live here with me, so we can be a real family."

"Does that mean you two will get married?" she asked, throwing us both for a loop. "Can I be the flower girl? Do I get to wear a white dress too? Oh! And I want pretty white ribbons in my hair. Will you let me wear makeup? Can—"

Shane broke out in a full belly laugh that had my heart lifting, whereas I was still stuck on the topic of marriage. Would he want to get married some day?

"Rosie, hold on," Shane started. "We're talking about moving in, right now. If this thing between all of us is going where I know it is, one day you'll get to be the most beautiful flower girl Jacksonville's ever seen."

Lana Rose bit her lip, a sign I had grown to recognize which meant she had something else she wanted to say.

"What is it, sweets?" I urged her.

"Does that make you my new mommy?" she practically whispered. "I—I know I called you that before, but saying it doesn't make it real."

My eyes welled up and I got up to go to her. Pulling a chair next to hers, I turned her toward me, then cupped her face between my hands.

"Lana Rose Peters, it would be an honor to be your mother. You are by far the best little girl anyone could ever hope for." I kissed her forehead.

Letting her go, she turned her chair to face her plate once more, grabbed her fork, and dug into her pancake. "Okay then," she said over her first mouthful of breakfast. "When do we move in?"

# forty-three

**EMBERLYN**

IT TOOK a week and two days before Nora was fully weaned off of the barbiturates that kept her in the induced coma; another few days before she began to show signs she might wake up. To say I was relieved would be an understatement. Shane had been edgy, waiting for results. It didn't help that Lana Rose had to be told about what was going on and asked at every turn when her grams would be coming home.

My side was healing nicely, but the tough part was the breathing exercises. The deep breaths I had to take every hour, and hold for a few seconds, stretched things out and were painful. However, within days of being home, I was noticing I could walk more than a few steps without feeling like I was being deprived of air.

Two weeks had gone by since a murderer lost his life, an innocent woman almost losing hers, and I'd found my life changing for the better.

Despite the fact Trevor had somehow managed to escape

Rex, Cade, and Brycen at the garage, I found myself embracing my new family life. Every morning, I woke with a smile on my face, wondering what the day would bring.

A knock at the door had me beaming with excitement. Mr. Carter was coming over for a visit with Mommy Devolin, while Dalton was at work.

"Rosie!" I called out as I headed for the entrance, taking care of the alarm, then the locks. Rushed footsteps announced her impending barrel down of the stairs.

"Coming!"

Opening the door, I greeted our guests with a smile—which fell promptly when I saw who stood there.

Seconds later, I was pushed back as Trevor made his way inside, slamming the door behind him.

"I'm done waiting," he growled.

"Rosie, get back upstairs!" I shouted out just as Trevor's fist connected with the side of my face, sending stars swimming in my vision.

"But—"

"Now, sweets, and lock your door!"

### SHANE

My cell rang just as I was about to sit down with Captain Dodge for my exit interview.

"Hello?"

"Daddy, something's wrong," Lana Rose announced. "Mommy yelled at me to get upstairs and lock my door."

That was the sign Emberlyn and I had agreed to give Rosie in case danger ever came knocking. If one of us wasn't in the house with her, she was to listen to the other, lock her door, and call the person that wasn't home. We'd practiced this process numerous times over the last week, what with the fact Sykes was still on the lam. It also went a long way to boost her courage.

"Calm down, honey," I told her. "I'm on my way. Do you know what's going on?"

"I heard the door slam, but that's it," she hiccupped. "What if it's that bad man again, Daddy?"

"It'll be okay, baby girl. Daddy's coming to help. Are Devolin and Carter there?"

"No. I thought that's who it was, because Mommy called me down, then yelled to get back upstairs."

"Okay. Stay in your room, keep the door locked, and I'll be there really soon." At that moment, I heard the crash of broken glass and a roar in the background. "Shit," I muttered. "Leaving the station right now, baby girl."

"O—okay, Daddy," she sniffled.

<h3 style="text-align:center">EMBERLYN</h3>

Who knew homemade pottery vases came in handy as weapons when yours was locked away in your bedside table?

The large urn-like vessel flew swiftly, deflected by Trevor's arm, only for it to shatter onto the wall next to his head, exploding in shards all over the place. Grabbing onto the next one from the same collection—this one bigger—I chucked it at him as hard as I could. This one he didn't have the chance to block. It made solid contact with his head, sending him down hard to the floor, where I watched his eyes roll back and close with a single hard bounce of his noggin on the tile flooring.

"I finally one-upped you, asshole," I spat, then made a mad dash up the stairs to my bedroom.

Grabbing the cordless phone by the bedside table, I fished my key out of my jewelry box, then unlocked the drawer. My Glock 26 sat in its case, loaded and ready to go. Slamming the drawer shut, I rushed out of my bedroom to Lana Rose's as I dialed.

"911, what is your emergency?"

"Intruder at…" I rattled off my address. "He's my ex-husband, who's just out of jail. He's already struck me, and I'm not sure how long he'll be out for. I—I hit him over the head with a vase."

"Okay, ma'am, someone's on their way. Can you keep the line open?"

"I—I…I have to check on my child. She's locked away in her room."

"Ma'am, I assure you she's safe there. The police are fifteen minutes out. Get yourself somewhere safe and hide out until they get there."

"But my daughter," I protested.

"Get somewhere safe," the woman ordered, just as I began to hear heavy footsteps climbing the stairs.

"Emmie, you shouldn't have done that," Trevor growled.

"I—I…gotta go," I called out and hung up just after hearing the dispatcher say, "Ma'am."

Dropping the phone to the floor, I took the same wide-legged stance Shane had shown me, blocking Trevor's access to Lana Rose's bedroom door. Taking aim at the top of the stair-well, I waited.

"Don't move!" I ordered my ex-husband as he reached the landing.

The man's face was bloody and swollen from my earlier hit, but his eyes indicated his faculties had returned and he was beyond pissed off.

*No more. Stand your ground, Em, this is ending right here, right now.*

Trevor laughed. "Are you going to shoot me, baby?"

I cringed. "If that's what it takes to make sure you leave me alone, once and for all, then yes."

Seconds felt more like hours as we stared each other down.

When he pounced, I closed my eyes and pulled the trigger. I fired two quick successive shots. The thump of a body hitting the floor had me looking to see what the damage was.

Where one of the bullets only entered his shoulder, the other one had hit Trevor in the gut. The fact he was now spitting up blood told me I'd done some serious damage, even though I'd only intended to stop him.

"You're done with your reign of terror, Trevor," I spat, my blood boiling that he'd forced my hand to shoot him, but mostly because he'd had a choice to leave me alone, and he'd chosen to make my life a living hell again. "You should have left me alone after you were sent to jail."

"Baby," he pleaded, "I need help. Call the ambulance," he coughed, a spatter of blood spraying out of his mouth as he did so. "I think I'm dying."

"It's more than what you deserve," I croaked, the reality of what I'd done hitting me all at once. "You should be locked away, and they should throw away the key for the way you've treated me."

"Emmie, please!" More coughing followed by wheezing. The pool of blood on the floor was growing quickly as the crimson fluid leaked out of his stomach, then followed gravity.

"Where was your mercy all of these years?" I cried, anger, bitterness, and despair ruling my emotions. "Why should I show you some when I never got the same in return?"

The man's lips moved, but no words came out. Crouching down beside him, all too aware that his life was slipping away, I showed him who I was to the core. Pressing my hands down on the wound in his stomach, I tried to slow the bleeding as I waited for the police to arrive, but it was no use. Blood oozed between my fingers, despite my efforts.

The scariest part of it all was over, but the part that would leave me with nightmares had come and gone within a mere minute: the look in Trevor's eyes and the last of his rasping breaths as they left his body would forever scar me.

# *forty-four*

**SHANE**

I PULLED up just as Devolin was arriving with the baby.

"What's going on?" she asked once she'd sized up the panicked look on my face.

"Stay here," I ordered. "Hell, get yourselves back in your car and lock it. Don't come out until I say so. Sykes is in there right now."

Her eyes rounded with understanding.

Just as sirens could be made out in the distance, I pulled my personal firearm out from its holster on my belt and made my way to the front door.

I was met with the sight of broken pottery and some blood on the entryway floor; but no one was in sight. The shuffling on the floor upstairs told me they were probably up there, but my police training kicked in, dictating I do the rounds of the main floor first to make sure Sykes wasn't laying in wait for me.

All cleared, I made my way toward the stairs.

What met me at the top had me breathing lighter, but the sight of Emberlyn undone tore at my heart.

"Sweetheart," I said, going down on a single knee to take Trevor's pulse.

"He's gone," she confirmed what I'd just discovered for myself. "I killed him."

Tucking my gun in its holster, I pulled her bloodied hands from the lifeless body she'd clearly tried to save and held them tightly in mine.

"Look at me," I said gently. She didn't. "I said, look at me, Em." My tone was harder this time. Commanding. When she did, I laid it on her. "You're not a killer. You defended yourself and our daughter the way you should have. You shot him in spots he was most likely to survive, like you were trained. Despite all the hell he's put you through over the years, you still tried to help him, sweetheart."

"I tried too late," she sobbed, collapsing into my chest. "I was so angry...so scared."

"I know, Em," I whispered against her hair, one of my hands cupping the back of her head, pressing her close to me. "But you couldn't have known this would happen."

She shook her head, no.

"Police!"

"Upstairs," I shouted back. "Perp is dead. Put your guns away, there's a child here."

A series of footsteps grew closer, and I peered up to find Will and Cap there, along with Greg and Emma, two other detectives I've worked with over the years.

"Son of a bitch," my soon-to-be-former-captain mumbled.

"Medics!"

"Upstairs. Scene is secure," Will hollered down. "One dead body, and..."

"Sweetheart, are you hurt?" I can't believe I forgot to ask, although the welt swelling on her cheek told me she at least had that.

"No. Just my face, but it's nothing ice won't cure," she mumbled.

"Just the dead body, guys," Will told them.

"Daddy?" we heard through the door to Lana Rose's bedroom.

"I'm here, baby girl," I told her. "I want you to stay in your room for a little bit longer, okay?"

"Is Mommy okay?"

Will seemed shocked by the statement, but both he and Captain Dodge grinned down at me with approval in their eyes after digesting my daughter's new moniker for Emberlyn.

"She's got a little bruise on her face, but she'll be fine."

"Okay..." A small pause. "Daddy?"

"Yeah?"

"Hurry up. I'm freaking out in here."

Some smirked at me, while others laughed lightly at the dramatic fashion my daughter chose to notify us of her state of mind. I only shook my head, grabbed Emberlyn by the elbows, and helped her up to her feet.

"Let's get you cleaned up, sweetheart."


### EMBERLYN


For the next few hours, I was subjected to photos, my clothes were taken away as evidence, and I'd had to recount my personal history, specifically my involvement with Trevor, along with what had happened earlier when he had shown up.

My ex's body had been taken away in a body bag and gurney almost straight away. By the time Shane and I had exited our bedroom, after he'd helped clean me up since shock was setting in, everything looked as it should have with the exception of the pool of congealing blood on the floor and the few scattered evidence number tags.

Lana Rose had been escorted downstairs by Will, who'd urged her to keep her eyes closed until he'd had her in the living room. I was glad to see she seemed no worse for wear, worried more about me than what she'd been through.

"When do we decorate for Christmas?" Lana Rose blurted out once all had calmed down. Shane was upstairs cleaning up as Devolin, Carter, and now Dalton sat with us on my large sectional.

The moment everyone had left earlier, Devolin rushed up to my snuggled-up form and dropped little Carter in my arms. I still had yet to let go of the sleeping baby and it had been an hour since they'd come in.

I looked over at Lana Rose, realizing Christmas was only a few weeks away and I had yet to do a stitch of decorating, a batch of baking, or any shopping for that matter.

Bending my head, I deposited a kiss to the little girl's crown as she cuddled into my side, playing gingerly with the baby's tiny hands until he'd grabbed onto one of her fingers.

"How about tomorrow?"

"Can we make cookies?" Her eyes glimmered with excitement.

"We can, and we can bring some to Grams when we go visit her," I told her. "Maybe the smell of my gingerbreads will make her so hungry that she'll finally wake up."

"Those are her favorites of yours," Rosie announced.

"Well then, we definitely need to make a few batches of them then, don't we?" The girl's head bobbed frantically in response, making the adults in the room, including myself, laugh.

# *forty-five*

LANA ROSE

## IT'S CHRISTMAS MORNING!

My eyes popped open, and I hurried to look at the clock. Mommy and Daddy told me that I needed to stay in bed until at least seven before I could get up. I was allowed to peek inside my stocking, but I wasn't to touch the gifts under the tree.

There were a lot of them! All different shapes and sizes; wrapped up in pretty paper that Mommy and I picked out, all on our own. She even let me help her wrap some of them, even though I didn't do as good of a job as she did with her gifts.

*7:05!*

That was my cue to get out of bed.

Rushing to the bathroom, I took a pee, then washed my hands. I reached for my toothbrush and put some paste on it. I didn't much like to brush my teeth, but it was Christmas, and I figured it would be a good gift to my parents if I took care of business without them having to remind me to do so. A spit, then a rinse, and a smile in the mirror later, I was good to go.

Tiptoeing downstairs, the tree we'd gone and cut, then

decorated with a mix of each other's decorations was lit and awaited me.

And so was the most humungous, most beautiful stocking —ever!

Giggling, I kneeled down on the rug and plunged my hand inside the larger-than-life sock and came out with my first trinket.

*Why is it wrapped?*

Santa never wrapped my stuffers up before.

My mind went back to when Sarah told me last week that Santa didn't exist. When I'd asked my parents, they'd told me he only exists for those who believe in him.

*Hmm... Maybe he decided to tease me this year because I doubted him?* Daddy didn't like doubt. He said that if we're strong people, we always know what to think, how to act, and what to believe in. It didn't matter what others thought. That's why I still believe in Santa.

Unwrapping the first trinket revealed a pack of gum.

"Oh, yay!" I cried out, then reached for the next little treasure which was also wrapped. *Silly Santa!*


"Merry Christmas, lovely girl of mine," Mommy whispered into my ear. I didn't hear her come downstairs, but I was glad everyone was finally up. That meant we were that much closer to the surprise.

Jumping up into my new mommy's arms and squeezing her neck until she giggled, I asked, "Where's Daddy?"

"He went to get Grams."

Yesterday was the best day ever, but I bet today would be better. Grams' doctor told us we could take her home. Because she has really bad headaches still, and gets woozy, the doctor said she couldn't be alone. That means she had to come stay with us.

"Merry Christmas, everyone!" Grams called, and I let Mommy go and ran to give Grams a hug. I missed hugging her.

All the gifts but one were opened, and paper littered the floor. I was bouncing on my knees, staring Daddy down so he could give me the go-ahead to give Mommy her gift.

"It's time, baby girl," he said.

"Time for what?" Mommy asked.

I rushed to my feet and ran to the tree to collect what Daddy and I had made. "Put your hand out," I told her, handing the item into her palm as soon as she did.

"What's this?" She inspected it with that artistic eye of hers. With the twinkle in her gaze, I knew she liked what she saw.

"Open it!" I hopped around. Why did adults have to take so long to open their gifts anyway?

"It opens?" Twirling the nut around in her hand, she must have noticed the tiny hinge on it. "Ah!"

Nestled inside the Christmas walnut Daddy and I decorated was the last piece that would make my dreams come true.

"Emberlyn Roth," Daddy said, his voice a little shaky. Daddy didn't do shaky; it was weird. "I know—"

"Yes!" she yelled out, then threw herself into my daddy, knocking them both down to the floor in fits of giggles as she kissed him silly, as Mommy likes to call it. Daddy does that a lot.

"You didn't let me finish," he grumbled beneath her, but kissed her back. I rolled my eyes. Them and their kisses. Even though I thought it was gross, I still felt happy when I saw them like that.

"Because I don't need those words, Shane," she explained. "I want to be your wife. I want to take care of our Lana Rose together, and—"

"And I want to have more babies...with you," Daddy whispered, "watch them grow up into great human beings because their mother is the best person in the world to teach them everything.”

“Shane,” she cooed.

*Oh no!* Mushy kisses were worse than silly kisses. “Guys!” I whined, Grams laughing in the background.

“Come here, baby girl,” Daddy said, and I listened.

When I got close enough, he pulled me down into their heap.

“Are you ready to be a princess for a day?” Mommy asked me.

I nodded. “I’m ready for you to be my real mommy.”

forty-six

EMBERLYN

I ADMIRED the twinkling of the ring on my left hand before taking one last glimpse in the mirror.

Wearing the red silk nightie I'd splurged on just last week, my hair hanging loose in blonde waves, I headed for the bathroom door.

Shane was sitting on the edge of the bed, sporting some goofy Christmas candy cane boxers, as he stowed away something in his bedside table as I exited.

His eyes rounded, his throat bobbed as he swallowed, and his underwear seemed to be pitching a candy cane of its own.

"Come here," he husked. I went. His hands reached for my hips, skimming the garment I wore. "You're beautiful, Em."

"Thank you." I cupped his cheek in my palm, the heat of his hands through the material warmed my blood; especially when his hands made a stop to squeeze and hold my ass.

"Tell me it's finally time, Em," he groaned, leaning his head into my stomach. "I need to make you mine again. It's been too long."

"Please, Shane," I practically begged. "I missed this part of us so much."

Flipping me as if I weighed nothing, I landed on my back atop the mattress, Shane's body covering mine.

"I missed this too, sweetheart, but I have to warn you..." His hands roamed as he slowly lifted my nightie, revealing the barely-there matching thong.

"What's that," I panted.

"I'm not feeling gentle right now."

I moaned. "Good." I didn't want gentle. I wanted Shane. Raw. Hot. Unfiltered.

"But first..."

Next thing I knew, I was flipped onto my stomach, Shane was sitting on the backs of my knees as he delivered a swift swat to my ass.

"Shane!" I squealed in shock more than in pain. Sure, there was a bit of discomfort, but the moment his hand rubbed over where he'd hit, the warmth from the smack triggered something dark...erotic...and fuck was I drenched.

"Stay still, Em, I'm thinking I like my handprint on that delicious ass of yours."

I groaned, my face planting into the sheets.

He delivered a slightly harder hit. A moan escaped my lips this time.

"I think someone likes this a little too much," Shane said, his hand rubbing my butt as I arched into his touch. He graced me with another swat, this one closer to my pussy lips before he forced his hands between my legs. "You're so wet for me, sweetheart."

"More," I pleaded. I swear, all he had to do was deliver a few more and I would explode. This was altogether a new thing for me.

Grabbing onto my thong, he pulled it roughly, snapping the elastic and tore them away from my body. "Spread your legs for me, Em. Make some room." Shane shuffled around to give me room to do so, my legs on the outside of his thighs as he kneeled between them.

He slapped me twice; one to each cheek in quick succession.

"I swear I'm going to come," I announced on a mewl.

His laugh was sultry, and next thing I knew, his mouth was on me, his hands spreading the sensitized skin of my ass cheeks as he licked, sucked and massaged that...

"Oh God, Shane, yes!" There was no penetration, only rubbing, but that move, in such a forbidden place, had me catapulting into bliss.

Before I'd recovered, Shane backed away, lifted my hips and plunged himself deep, taking my breath away.

"Fuck, yeah," he grunted between thrusts. "I really love my handprint on your ass, sweetheart. Feel that." He pulled out and pistoned back in. "Feel me, Em."

"I do!" I cried out, another surge overcoming me.

His hips kept their rhythm, strong and steady. "I want to feel you everywhere."

"Yes!"

"Your mouth...your pussy...fuck, I never thought I'd say this, but I want your ass, Em." As he said it, his thumb came to play with that tiny rosette, and I felt myself get even closer to the edge. "Fuck, she likes that."

"Mm-hmmphf," I managed.

The moment his thumb breached that tight ring, I exploded on a loud keening wail into the mattress.

"That's right, Em...milk my cock." He hissed. "So fucking good. So close."

Spent, I could only let him use me like I wanted him to. It took him a few more thrusts and then he buried himself to the hilt, grinding into me as he spilled himself on a roared bite into my shoulder.

**SHANE**

"Mine," I growled, showering Emberlyn's back with a slew of sloppy kisses as I made love to her skin from the back of her neck down to her tailbone.

Her body shook with her pleasure. "Yours," she moaned.

"I want you again," I confessed, helping her roll onto her back, then removing the rest of her nightie. "I want you in every way I could possibly ever have you."

Her arms stretched up, then fell to grasp onto the slats of her headboard, while her legs lifted to wrap around my hips. "Show me," she said, her eyes fused to mine.

Hovering over her, I bent down low and snagged her mouth with mine and proceeded to do as she'd asked.


"Thank you," I whispered up to the ceiling, Emberlyn cuddled into my side as one of her hands played with mine.

She lifted her head to look at me, depositing a sweet kiss to my pec. "What are you thanking me for now?"

"For being you...making my daughter happy...giving me everything I need." I eyed her glistening eyes. "Thank you for bringing me back to the land of the living...for showing me happiness can still exist, even after a loss so horrific. Thank you for loving me."

"I can't wait to be your wife, Mr. Peters," she whispered on a smile.

"Let's not wait to get married," I said, rolling her onto her back, leaning over her. "I have the urge to see you round with my child."

Emberlyn giggled. "I'm pretty sure we don't need to be married to have a baby, Shane." She gave me a meaningful look, lifting her head to kiss my lips. "But you're right...I don't want to wait either."

"Merry Christmas, my beautiful Em," I whispered.

"Merry Christmas, Shane."

*epilogue*

EMBERLYN

THE SUN WAS SHINING, the breeze was light as I wandered around the grounds. Beautiful weeping willows surrounded the plot where my feet came to a halt. It couldn't have been a more perfect place to be laid to rest.

Crouching down, I handled the precious package in my arms with care, reading the inscription before me.

*Eva Peters — Loving mother, wife, and best friend. You will always live in our hearts. 1979-2007.*

I'd been here numerous times before. I'm not sure as to why I felt the need to come back, aside from the fact I felt like I owed it to Shane's first wife to show her I was taking care of those she loved most when she now couldn't.

"Hi, Eva," I whispered, "I know it's been a little while since I've last stopped by, but I came as soon as I could." Looking down at the bundle in my arms, I couldn't help the prideful smile. "I'd like you to meet Asher Peters. He was born last week, on your birthday of all days. He's got Shane's eyes and temper." I laughed. "I'm not sure where he gets the black hair from, but I like to think it was your way to stay in our family." I sighed. "I know I've said it so many times before but thank you for allowing me to care for Rosie and Shane. Next time, I promise I'll bring the entire family with me."

Fifteen minutes went by before Asher cued for his next feeding. Regaining my feet, I bent down, kissed my fingers, and pressed them to Eva's name.

"Happy belated birthday, beautiful angel."

### SHANE

Over the last year, I'd wondered where Emberlyn would sometimes disappear to. It was never for a lengthy period of time—usually an hour at the most—but she'd always come back to me, looking for cuddles.

I always sensed her sadness beneath the joy she seemed to always radiate.

Today, something told me to follow her—call it intuition, or a gut feeling—so I did; all the way to the cemetery I'd taken her to once after our engagement. It's where we'd buried Eva ten years ago.

I watched from a distance as Emberlyn cuddled Asher while she talked to Eva. Like night and day both women were. Despite the devastation I'd felt at losing Eva, losing her had brought me to Emberlyn and a life I could have only dreamed of living once upon a time.

As soon as my wife had set our son in the stroller and turned to leave, her eyes met mine, then her steps halted. That's when I made my approach.

"Busted, huh?" she mumbled shyly, tilting her head downward to avoid my scrutinizing. I smiled. "Are you mad?"

Tilting her face up so she could look into my eyes, I leaned in and kissed her forehead.

"Mad?" I shook my head. "No, I'm not mad. I'm in awe of you, Em."

"I've been coming here at least once a month since you first brought me here with Rosie," she confessed.

"It all makes sense now," I told her, and wrapped my arm around Emberlyn's shoulders. "Need a cuddle?"

She shrugged. "I'll never refuse your cuddles."

"Come on." I ushered her toward the car as she pushed the stroller along. "We have a date to get ready for, and a daughter who's chomping at the bit to feed her baby brother in order to help her grams. And don't get me started on Grams; she says we've been keeping him to ourselves far too much." That gained me one of those giggles I loved so much.

Having buckled Asher into his seat, I folded and stored the stroller into the back of the car, then headed to open up Emberlyn's door. She paused before getting in, cupping my face in her hands, and brushed my nose with hers.

"I love you, Shane Peters," she whispered over my lips before depositing a sweet kiss.

"And I love you, Emberlyn Peters."

Forever.

Always.

Until the end of time.

---

If you enjoyed *Night Shift*, please take a moment to let other readers know what you thought of Shane, little Lana Rose, and Emberlyn's journey by leaving a review at your favorite retailer, or visit Goodreads. Thank you!

Born and raised in small town Northern Ontario, Canada, award—winning author, Carey Decevito has had a penchant for reading and writing for as long as she can remember.

A writer of erotic romance, paranormal romance, and romantic suspense, this lover of food will throw in a bit of heat, a dash of sass, a pinch of comedy, and a dollop of real—life experience in order to provide her readers with a story that will mess with their emotions from start to finish.

Family and friends are her lifeblood, but Carey also enjoys conquering the outdoors, sports, traveling, and playing tourist in Canada's National Capital region. When life gets crazy, she seeks respite through her writing and submersing herself in the latest addition to her library. If all else fails, she knows there's never a dull moment with her two daughters, her goofy husband, and their dog who she swears is out to get her.

She is the author of *The Broken Men Chronicles* series, the *Essence Extracted* trilogy, and the *Nightshade* series.

For more book updates, visit
www.careydecevitobooks.com
or by subscribing to her newsletter!

facebook.com/carey.writes

instagram.com/carey_decevito

x.com/ItalRT4u

bookbub.com/authors/carey-decevito

amazon.com/author/careydecevito